Forbidden Technology

Propellantless Propulsion, Anti-Gravity, Anti-Inertia, Overunity Free Energy

Revealed

by

Robert Francis

In a science fiction thriller set in modern America, a male alcoholic stoner obsessed with faster than light travel must evade and outsmart the near omniscient Project Luddite and It's All Seeing Eye to see his dream come true. - Forbidden Technology - Propellantless Propulsion, Anti-Gravity, Anti-Inertia, and Overunity Free Energy Revealed by Robert Francis

Prologue

You may have come across this novel in many ways, I distributed business cards with my website hosting the book for free to many people, I sent out mass emails to addresses all over the country or you may have purchased it from Amazon.

Tom DeLonge's launch of To the Stars Academy which includes attempting to engineer space time and study electrogravitics has given me the courage to finally publish this novel. Electrogravitics is one name for the propellantless propulsion technology mentioned in this novel. The **Forbidden Technology** I present in this novel is **real**. It is my goal to put this knowledge into the popular consciousness. Having millions read my novel through the mass email and fake torrents is not enough. We need to break into the mainstream media.

There is one way to do this that I believe will have the most success and I ask you to please do it.

The way to break into the mainstream media is to make it to the New York Times bestseller list. That requires 9,000 books sold in a week. We need to stay on that list for as long as possible. The longer this book is on the NY Times bestseller list the more difficult it will be for the government to pretend this technology does not exist and to suppress experimenters from creating their own working prototypes.

My goal is for this technology to become known and used, a part of everyday life.

What I need from you the reader is if you enjoy the novel or just want to make this technology public please buy the ebook from Amazon.

We need to break into the NY Times bestseller list, I fear this is the only way the government will admit to the existence of the technology or at the least not harass and murder those seeking to prove the technology works.

Please, share this novel with everyone you know. If they like it or want to make this technology public encourage them to buy the novel on Amazon. All it takes is 9,000 ebooks sold in a week to get onto the NY Times list.

At this point in time I am on food stamps and Medicaid, I don't have the money at the moment to start creating prototypes of the technology in the novel. I call on you the reader to prove that it works with videos to be released on Youtube and other platforms. I will join you when I have more money either from ebook sales or launching a successful freelance computer programming career. I have thrown my hat over the wall for creating the flying car.

I hope all of you will throw your hats over the wall too, thank you.

Chapter 1 – Will it work or will it not.

"Time to put up or shut up."

I made my way into the abandoned field.

Visible on the ground is a Biefeld-Brown flat parallel plate capacitor, in other words a large sandwich with a sheet of G10 dielectric on the bottom, a sheet of copper plate, another sheet of G10 dielectric, another sheet of copper plate and finally another sheet of G10 dielectric. Epoxy resin encompasses the entire parallel plate capacitor device. The outer G10 dielectric sheets and epoxy resin keeps the electricity contained within the object so it doesn't short out to the ground or me.

Cables came off both plates to the top of two Marx generators. In essence voltage multipliers that dramatically raises the voltage from the four 30 kV flyback transformers to -1Megavolt on the negative Marx generator leading to the negative plate and +1Megavolt on the positive Marx generator leading to the positive plate.

The electricity arcs between each stage of the Marx Generator, delivering a pulsed voltage output into the flat parallel plate capacitor. It starts off with a voltage applied to a trigatron which takes the place of the first stage's arc gap which sends a voltage pulse into the Marx generator and through the rest of the arc gaps. With properly spaced arc gaps at each stage of the generator and a trigatron triggering the first stage, electricity can be pulsed through the Marx Generators hundreds of times a second.

The four 30kV flyback transformers are connected through a mosfet circuit which takes in 120V AC current and outputs 170V AC into the flyback transformers. The mosfet circuit is plugged into an inverter which converts my overunity free energy generators 12V DC to 120V AC.

I couldn't help but wonder if the prototype device would work. I had spent considerable amounts of money and time to test a hypothesis that most of the science world would say wouldn't work. I guess it was a mix of curiosity, hope, and obsession that had propelled me, some evidence from others who conducted experiments on flat parallel plate capacitors, along with cynicism that if the government did have the technology they would keep it secret.

Heck, parking lots have few entrances and exits precisely to control traffic and help security capture shop lifters. How would they begin to deal with flying cars? There are no spike strips in the sky, how would police who were chasing a fugitive pull the fugitive over if he decided to run. Perhaps the government already has tractor beam technology that could stop a fleeing vehicle but that is only a guess, I have seen no evidence of tractor beam technology.

"Regardless, all I have to do is throw the switch, either it will work or it won't. Worrying about it won't change anything."

It feels like yesterday that I saw the Disclosure Project press briefing video that changed my life forever. Some of the people in it have gotten a lot of flack, reputations left tattered, some possibly deserving, others not. But in my eyes the main character of that story was a guy named Mark McCandlish.

Chapter 2 - Wetworks

Agent Gamma, Michael Sizemore, and Agent Zeta, Thomas Philips, were in position. They were on an assassination mission, tasked by Project Luddite to murder a potential threat to the established order or as it is often referred to, National Security. Agent Gamma used his lock picking equipment to open the front door and made his way into the apartment of the target. With him was a syringe of heavy metals: uranium, thorium, platinum, barium, aluminum, beryllium, and lithium. The target was a man by the name of James Allen Higgens. Agent Zeta was tailing the target who was running errands ensuring he didn't come home in the middle of Agent Gamma's operation which would have turned his simple mission into ugly home invasion turned murder. The target was making a documentary, **The Truth Denied: Zero Point & the Alien Reproduction Vehicle**: **https://www.youtube.com/watch?v=I4J9RYUlp9o** about forbidden propulsion and energy technology from a man he was interviewing, Mark McCandlish.

It was feared Higgens' documentary would catch on and open many people's eyes about various forbidden technologies that his superiors at Project Luddite were so diligently trying to keep suppressed. If the documentary caught on fire knowledge of the forbidden technologies would become much more widely known and impossible to continue to keep suppressed. The decision was made to take him out before he could finish the documentary.

By poisoning the target it would appear that he died of natural causes rather than murdered which might turn him into a martyr and make the popularity of his documentary soar. They considered shooting him with the heart attack gun, a weapon they've had in their arsenal for a long time that shoots a tiny frozen dart of poison that mimics a heart attack: **http://www.youtube.com/watch?v=BSEnurBApdM**but the decision was made that sabotaging his food by injecting it with toxic cancerous heavy metals would be better as he was physically in good shape. Agent Gamma proceeded from the entrance of the apartment into the kitchen. Agent Gamma opened the refrigerator door and found some meat that would make for a perfect delivery system. Agent Gamma took out a package of hamburger injecting it with the syringe of heavy metals. The concentration of metals should cause a rapidly progressing cancer in the target. Agent Gamma then proceeded to exit the apartment, radioing to Agent Zeta that his mission was complete. Agent Zeta stopped tailing the target and proceeded back to base.

Two months later James Allen Higgens was dead, contracting a rare fast acting form of bile duct cancer, his documentary incomplete. While incomplete it was still released as is by Higgens' financial backer, heavy metals in his system only known because his family and the financial backer insisted on an autopsy: **http://www.paradigmresearchgroup.org/graphics/AllenToxicologyReport.pdf**

The performance of an autopsy was not anticipated by Project Luddite nor was its release to the public, on the internet. It did not however appear to catapult the documentary into the public eye, the documentary only receiving a few thousand viewers. The mission appeared to be successful, the forbidden technology was still relatively unknown, kept from the public as it would be indefinitely by Project Luddite.

Chapter 3 – How it All Began

I walked over to the nightstand to grab my bong packing it with some mid grade cannabis and took a couple hits. I walked back to my home office (one should never smoke near display screens, it gives them a yellow tint) with the **Disclosure Project** video playing. There is a diagram of something called the ARV being held up to the cameras.

"Woah woah woah, let's back up."

I look at the URL to bookmark it, **http://www.youtube.com/watch?v=lkswXVmG4xM**. I roll the time back to the beginning of the man's testimony. His name is **Mark McCandlish** and the name of the vehicle is the **Alien Reproduction Vehicle** or **ARV** also nicknamed the **Flux Liner**. The Disclosure Project video did not give too much information on how the vehicle operated other than it operated on zero point energy whatever that meant. I was determined to find out as much information on Alien Reproduction Vehicle as possible.

I immediately conducted some searches of those keywords and found a wikia link. It was an interview with Mark McCandlish, telling his story and how he came across it. Apparently a friend of his named Brad Sorenson was supposed to go to an air show with McCandlish. McCandlish had to back out due to last minute work with Popular Science to create the cover art for next month's issue.

Sorenson ran into a friend at the air show, supposedly a former defense secretary rumored to be Frank Carlucci. Carlucci took Sorenson to see some of the more restricted parts of the air show, not knowing about all the top secret vehicles that would be in the hanger near by for show to some special politicians in the area.

Sorenson saw a few prototype aircraft but the big surprise was the ARV. It was floating above the floor with no apparent landing gear. Some panels on the side of the craft had been removed allowing Sorenson to see some of the components of the vehicle.

At the bottom of the vehicle about 11-12 inches thick were 4 layers of flat parallel plate capacitors with half inch thick copper plates, cut into thin pizza pie slices encased in some sort of plastic or epoxy resin. Sorenson was told that half a million to a million volts are dumped into these capacitors.

The capacitors supposedly provided the pushing force that propels the craft upwards. When a flat parallel plate capacitor is charged it lifts towards its positive plate. This is known as the Biefeld-Brown effect.

Around the middle of the vehicle was a large plastic casting that had a large set of copper coils. The coil was about 18 inches thick at the top, 8-9 inches in height with 15-20 layers of coils. The purpose of this coil was unstated. I wasn't sure what its purpose might be, a device to ionize air around the craft reducing wind resistance?

The power source possibly involved mercury but the details on that were very sketchy, the diagram and cutaways did not show that component of the vehicle. It was stated that it was a power amplifier. With so little to go on I didn't figure I'd ever uncover the technology behind the energy generator in the ARV.

I immediately started doing more research.

Chapter 4 – Debunking the Debunkers

I made my way from my bedroom where I had just steamrolled several hits of cannabis off of my bong, getting nice and high, to my home office. I went to Google first, I found an article called **How I Control Gravitation** by Thomas Townsend Brown. It discusses an experiment of his using two 44lb lead spheres suspended by a wire, positive for one sphere, negative for the other sphere with a glass rod in between the spheres. When 120kV of steady DC electricity was turned on Brown claims the apparatus moved in the direction from negative sphere to positive sphere.

Now there are lifter builders out there who will claim the Biefeld-Brown effect is nothing more than ion wind, electrically charged air, and that air flow is what lifts the craft into the air. They have even put lifters in a vacuum to show the propulsion effect will not work without air and would therefore be useless in the vacuum of space. Lifters are missing what appears to be a critical component, the dielectric between the positive and negative plates, in this example the glass rod or in the ARV the plastic, G10, or epoxy resin.

Otherwise, for there to be movement of the 44lb spheres, Brown's lab would had to have a hurricane blowing through it. That does not seem likely. Occam's Razor says the simplest reason is the most likely one, even if that reason defies the known laws of physics. The experimental data trumps theory.

Further research was required though.

I found one paper, **Twenty First Century Propulsion Concept: http://www.otherhand.org/wp-content/uploads/2012/04/Talley-paper-propulsion-concept.pdf**, in the Anomalies section, a series of experiments with pulsed voltages was done.

Generally, no motion of the test devices was observed, except in Test No. 69 (the last test) where a very small but detectable motion was seen.

The only experiment producing a result was when the 19kV was applied to the positive plate at a pulse rate frequency of 600 Hz with a solid dielectric between the capacitor plates that caused the torsion pendulum to twist ever so slightly, applying a small but consistent pressure.

I took another break to smoke some more cannabis from my bowl. I calmly watched the smoke fill the room as I exhaled. Euphoria and certainty that I was onto something filled my mind like the smoke in the room.

Another paper, **Asymmetrical Capacitors for Propulsion:**
https://ntrs.nasa.gov/archive/nasa/casi.ntrs.nasa.gov2004171929.
pdf, in the Observations section detailed one of the experiments
where movement was seen in a vacuum. Only the capacitor with a
solid dielectric between the positive and negative capacitor plates
moved in a vacuum when the 50kV steady DC was first applied to
the positive capacitor plate. A rotation of about 1/8th was seen
through the viewing port of the vacuum chamber. A spark
accompanied the movement which stopped just after it started.

The conductors of the experiment speculated that material had been
ejected when the spark occurred and that that was why the capacitor
moved. That seems unlikely to me, after all, why weren't there
sparks and material ejected when the other capacitors were tested?
Furthermore, if they had encased the Brown capacitor with epoxy
that would have eliminated the spark and they would have been able
to tell if the Brown capacitor would have still moved.

The key appears to be high voltage, the higher the better, those last
two experiments used 19kV and 50kV, Brown used 120kV steady
DC, and the ARV supposedly used between 500kV – 1,000kV DC,
pulsed into the capacitors.

Chapter 5 – Fun with Friends

I was unemployed collecting unemployment. This left my schedule
wide open, my mornings asleep, and my nights long. I didn't wake
and bake, that wasn't for me. When I did get up, I spent what was for
me mornings, working on an ecommerce site, attempting to sell
electronics drop shipped from the distributor directly to the

customer's home. The product feed they had was enormous and full of errors or blank information. I attempted to create some software to process the feed and extract significant details like the resolution of a TV or megapixels of a camera. During this time I would be chatting on AOL's instant messenger network, using the open source pidgin program with my friend Gary or Meg. Besides chatting over AIM or playing video games, watching movies/TV and collecting the biggest most organized porn collection in the world, I was working on this feed processor from the time I got up till the time I went out to get a few drinks with my friend Steve.

I visited my friend Steve several times a week at various bars, Pepe's (not Frank Pepe's) in Manchester, Hooters in Manchester, the brew pub next door. We got soused a lot of the time. We liked to think we were better at computer systems drunk than others were sober. For him it was true, me, not so much.

We talked a lot about Steve's job and the chaos and infighting that was rampant there. We talked about the ARV though he didn't seem to have a belief on it one way or another. After a good dinner and plenty of beer I often joined my other friends in Middlefield.

There we drank and smoked cannabis. I found if I was sufficiently drunk I usually did not get paranoid. We joked around about TV shows and movies, we played beer pong and lit the outdoor fire pit. I had anxiety but for the most part I was fine inebriated. I was single and most of my friends were not. Shamefully at times I found myself attracted to my friends girlfriends.

We mixed up partners in beer pong and had our wins and losses which always involved drinking more beer so no one ever really lost. My friend Gary had a foul shot like approach to his beer pong throwing. Dustin would try and slip a bounce by his opponent hoping for two cups. Chris was a solid shot maker and a joker. Scott and Jessica often left the party together early, retiring to their apartment. Scott was an engineer and had some interest in the material I had come across but none of it fit in with his education and training. None of the rest really seemed like they would be interested in the ARV story but I did send Scott a few messages through Facebook about articles I found related to the ARV and the technology.

Getting home at 3am in the morning I would pack up the bong and get stoned for hours browsing the web, playing video games like Bridge Commander (sure of myself that I would make a good Captain) Star Trek Armada 2, Diablo 2, watching TV like Buffy the Vampire Slayer, the various Star Trek TV series, Stargate SG-1, or movies like Star Wars or more porn, or all three till the sun came up.

Smoking cannabis a lot was my vice, I smoked alone all the time, drinking was more a social thing for me, some might say I had an alcohol problem too. I didn't drink by myself nor drink the next morning to get rid of the hair of the dog but I had had a couple blackouts and plenty of hangovers.

Chapter 6 – Project Luddite

It was Bill Armstrong's job to oversee the INFOSEC department of Project Luddite, an unacknowledged special access program within Homeworld Security, another unacknowledged special access program few in government even know about with the exception of certain members of the Executive branch and the **Gang of Eight**: **https://en.wikipedia.org/wiki/Gang_of_Eight_(intelligence)** in

Congress. Not even Edward Snowden, the NSA whistle blower employed by Booz Allen a big government contractor, knew of or had access to it. It was Armstrong's job to make sure certain propulsion, energy generation, nanotechnology, and artificial intelligence discoveries remain undiscovered for the foreseeable future. The U.S. government principally and the other permanent members of the U.N. Security council do not feel the world is ready for true flying cars, unlimited energy, nanobots in our bloodstreams and brain, or sentient AI.

This meant using the NSA's upstream data processing to scour through all the information passing through the entire electronic communications systems of the earth: internet, phone systems, text messaging, CCTV camera visual and audio feeds; and watch for anyone looking into these technologies and depending on their level of progress towards achieving, understanding, or building these technologies, refer them to the higher ups in Project Luddite to decide how to deal with them and if it is determined, to their OPSEC wetworks unit.

Armstrong wasn't crazy about the mission of Project Luddite but felt it was necessary. He was a practical man and the restricted technologies represented too much of an unknown as to how they would change the world.

Biefeld-Brown propulsion would making flying cars an actual practical form of transportation. It would be far faster and safer assuming it was all computer controlled like the plans for AI driven Tesla and Google cars. But terrorists could use them to make flying bombs to smash into skyscrapers. Of course terrorists could do the same with small planes or drones right now. The potential chaos if things weren't meticulously planned and rolled out could be high.

Unlimited overunity free energy would crash the various energy industries and the massive investments the top 1% have: oil, gas, coal, nuclear, wind, and solar. Energy comprised a huge proportion of the global economy and oil is largely traded in dollars making America's currency the default world currency, artificially strengthening our dollar.

Nanotechnology could harm people's brains or other health. It could be used to create dangerous viruses or toxic materials. They could stop hearts or cause brain aneurysms. With enough sophistication who knows if they could take control of people and force them to commit acts they otherwise wouldn't.

A sentient rogue AI could conceivably take advantage of broken software to install itself on every computer's firmware in the world making it impossible to get rid of. If it jumps air gaps on defense mainframes it could take control of military hardware.

Armstrong knew his mission was vital and he did his duty with distinction.

Chapter 7 – Curiosity Knows No Bounds

After my initial research into the ARV I could not get the idea, the potential technologies, out of my head. I was flat out obsessed with the ARV. My head swimming from smoking cannabis, I browsed the web looking for anything I could find on the Biefeld-Brown effect. The euphoria of the cannabis along with the idea that faster than light travel is more possible and practical than I ever thought during my days of watching Star Trek: The Next Generation gave me a constant high, well along with the cannabis.

It didn't stop there, I started researching subjects who might have been in the know. Ben Rich a Lockheed CEO supposedly made the claim that "we now have the technology to bring ET home". That implies we have interstellar propulsion technology, energy technologies to power the propulsion systems, shielding to protect the craft from radiation, X-rays, gamma rays, cosmic rays. I wanted to be Star Trek's Zephram Cochran, the man in Star Trek who created warp drive and brought faster than light travel to his fellow humanity on earth, something I could potentially still do considering the government has shown no indication that it intends to release the technology.

A Lockheed senior scientist by the name of Boyd Bushman made the claim that two magnets with their north poles forced and bolted together fell slower than an equivalent weight rock in a test he conducted inside a tall Lockheed building. Somehow this field put out by the two magnets bolted together reduced the effect of gravity on the magnetic object. A puzzle, it didn't immediately occur to me the usefulness of this discovery, it wasn't a propulsive effect after all, but I kept it on the back burner in my mind as an experiment that proved gravity's effects could be altered.

I ran across information on a GE engineer Henry William Wallace who claimed that odd nuclear spin material like Bismuth were needed to produce a propulsive effect. His rather convoluted example involved two rotating discs. When one was rotated in one direction the other disc right next to it rotated in the opposite direction without any motor turning it. Somehow the second disc was affected by the first rotating disc. Copper also has an odd nuclear spin, weaker than certain isotopes of Titanium, or Bismuth, so perhaps an odd nuclear spin material in the capacitor plates was needed to propel the ARV. A research paper on Heim theory, a little known theory developed decades ago and expanded on in a new research paper postulated that odd nuclear spin material used in a rotating disc with a perpendicular electromagnetic field would feel a propulsive effect parallel with the magnetic field. Another couple tidbits I kept in my mind.

A man by the name of Bruce DePalma stated that his homopolar generator produced overunity electricity. His experiment didn't show that though. But it was possible that his crude tools, an ordinary magnetic coil rather than superconducting, very low voltage and high current, and carbon brushes instead of liquid mercury contacts all worked together to decrease the machine's efficiency. He stated clocks lost seconds that were near the device while his control clock kept normal time. And perhaps most important he supposedly got a call from George Bush that he better watch what he is doing or he would get his head blown off. Because of this he moved to Australia. He however turned to using a steel disc instead of an odd nuclear spin material like copper and never made a working model.

I ran across a JASON paper on using a homopolar generator as a fast electricity delivery system. It included a 10 Tesla magnetic coil and counter rotating plates within the magnetic field to boost the voltage to 50kV. The ARV had an enormous coil around the middle of the craft. Perhaps this specific type of homopolar generator was the power plant of the ARV, an overunity device? Regardless, it would not be easy to reproduce.

There's a man by the name of Eugene Podkletnov who supposedly discovered an anti-gravity effect with a rotating superconductor in a perpendicular electromagnetic field. With sufficient rotational acceleration a decrease of gravity would occur above the superconductor plate. Another thing to keep mind of but it sounds too complicated and expensive to reproduce in the garage and it was only a partial effect, not strong enough for any kind of practical use. That said it might be possible to generate the same effect using discs made of odd nuclear spin material and it might be possible to increase the levitation effect by increasing the rotational speed of the disc and strength of the magnetic field.

Chapter 8 – Wisdom of the Crowd

I had finished the feed processor to my satisfaction ripping all the attributes of a product into a Google Products compatible feed. As I said though, the feed contained many errors and the prices left little room for profit. I decided to build a spidering tool to spider the distributor's website for product information that was missing in the feed. I was using php and making http connections was a little tricky, I was a little out of my depth but managed to build the spidering tool. It sped up the manual work so much that my friend Gary asked me to provide him feeds from it as well.

I couldn't talk to my friends about the research and after smoking cannabis and obsessing about the technology, I couldn't keep it to myself. I started posting to various UFO forums like Above Top Secret, Reality Uncovered, and other lesser known sites. Few seemed interested in what I uncovered. Most posts stated that it wouldn't work for whatever reason. On Above Top Secret, one of the forum veterans stated that the government did not care if people knew about the technology but they did care about people trying to prove it was real.

Reality Uncovered especially tried to dissuade me from pursuing the technology. One of the commentators, a forum admin, stated that it appeared I wanted to prove whether the tech would work instead of leaving it to Mark McCandlish. I enthusiastically encouraged the forum participants to conduct experiments. People mostly wanted to discuss flying triangles. It was as if the ARV was not well known or considered not real.

To make things even weirder, floods of posts would occur in the forum when I created my thread. At other times the forum was mostly quiet but when I posted on one subject or another relating to the ARV or Biefeld-Brown people seemed to come out of the woodwork.

I started to get paranoid that some entity was trying to suppress what I was writing, bury it in a sea of posts. Could the government really have such an operation? Was I really onto something? Where there is smoke there is fire, I couldn't dismiss what had happened so easily.

I decided to try and see if the government did in fact have programs to bury threads in forums.

A few quick Google searches turned up stories of paid commentators on blog posts and forum threads who were there strictly to try and sway public opinion to the mainstream media vision of America. If they are doing this much about political issues one can only imagine what they are doing to sway opinions on highly classified technologies.

Further research found a discussion of COINTELPRO tactics that were used to bury posts on forbidden technology.

Technique 1 – Forum Sliding

If a post contained any forbidden technologies Project Luddite monitored it can quickly be buried down the list of posts in the forum with a technique known as **forum sliding**. Many forums contain old threads that pop up from time to time. Additional posts to these threads can be done by a few members or even one poster using multiple accounts with 1-2 line posts that add no real value and whose only purpose is to move the forbidden post down the page of the forum where it is less likely to be seen.

Technique 2 – Consensus Cracking

Another effective technique to control the conversation is consensus cracking. It involves posting a very weak post in favor of the original post but with little evidence and facts backing up the post leading people to dismiss the post and with it the original post.

Technique 3 – Topic Dilution

Topic dilution is a technique used in forum sliding but has additional uses. By continually posting non-related posts to the thread topic it causes Resource Burn. The off topic posts prevent any kind of real productive conversation from happening in the thread as it gets buried with gossip talk. The conversation turns away from facts and evidence and towards opinion and baseless speculation.

Technique 4 – Information Collection

COINTELPRO agents looking to see what people know, volunteer something they know about a topic that maybe close to the line of being true about a forbidden technology in an effort to get the target to reveal all he knows. This gives agents a way to get a better idea on what people know for targets that are more guarded.

Chapter 9 – Debunking the TR-3B Flying Triangle

All my research to date has shown that a flying triangle of some sort probably exists. There have been too many sightings by civilians reported to authorities like local law enforcement for it to not exist. However there is not a single picture of the TR-3B flying triangle which does cast doubt on the existence of the craft. I am however fairly certain that the TR-3B flying triangle of Ed Fouche fame is, in my opinion, disinformation.

For one, Ed Fouche stated the TR-3B had a rotating crew compartment. Why would a craft need such a complicated device? It doesn't make any sense. Moving parts fail so it stands to reason that any kind of flying craft would use as few of such parts as possible. It sounds cool but it would be a big technological hassle with no real apparent gains.

The TR-3B supposedly had a mercury centrifuge that compressed and ionized the mercury into a plasma under 250,000 atmospheres of pressure with the mercury rotating at 50,000 rpm inside the centrifuge. This centrifuge. surrounded the crew compartment and supposedly reduced gravity's effect on the TR-3B by 90%. Nothing about it affecting inertia as well was stated. I am in no position to know if a centrifuge. capable of that much pressure could be created, nor do I know if a mercury plasma could be rotated inside a centrifuge. at such a high speed, and finally I do not know if it would reduce gravity. I do know that it is not at all reproducible by the average experimenter in his garage.

Lastly it was said there are solid oxide rockets in the three corners of the triangle. Rockets would require frequent refueling and they would make noise, virtually all sightings of flying triangles say they run silent. Those two facts directly contradict each other. I am more likely to believe the reported sightings than the tale of one government worker.

I think Ed Fouche was a disinformationist who was tasked with putting out the story on the TR-3B flying triangle to get UFO enthusiasts to focus on a UFO tale that has no experimental value for the average garage tinkerer unlike the Alien Reproduction Vehicle.

Lastly, Ed Fouche admitted years after his story in a drunken video that he was a big liar. How can his story be trusted when he admits to being a liar.

Chapter 10 – Debunking the Bob Lazar Sport Model UFO

Again, I cannot say whether or not the Bob Lazar story of the Sport Model UFO is real but it appears to me to distract from more relevant stories like the ARV.

Bob Lazar stated he worked on a base nearby Area 51 called S4. While he was supposedly there he worked on one of the UFOs there called the Sport Model which was a UFO given to us by aliens, possibly the Greys. The Sport Model UFO supposedly ran on element 115, generating its power and creating the gravity waves the craft ran on. A stable isotope of this element does not exist on earth. There may or may not be a stable isotope of element 115 with the right number of neutrons, and somewhere in the universe it might exist and be a minable resource but again, it does not exist on earth.

He claims that there are two forms of gravity which he called Gravity A and Gravity B. One being the normal force of gravity we are familiar with and the other a currently unknown force.

He has been given credence by some who say he precisely timed a visit to the outskirts of Area 51 with some friends while a craft was seen zipping around the sky.

However, again we have a UFO tale that leaves nothing for the garage tinkerer to experiment with. There are no explanations as to how the craft works, it all comes down to element 115.

Lazar claimed to have attended universities that have no record of his enrollment. I do not think the government could erase a person's past in this way. What about his teachers, his fellow students, surely there would be people there who would know him. Perhaps a yearbook photo if he got his picture taken. Yet he can't point to a single person or piece of evidence to backup his claims of the schools he attended.

Furthermore he was recorded going to a technical university in California, a college across the country from the ones he claimed to have attended at the same time.

Regardless of the validity of the Sport Model UFO tale, it has no practical value in determining how UFO's fly, no practical explanations as to how it flies, how it can be replicated, unlike the Alien Reproduction Vehicle.

Chapter 11 – Information Suppression

It had been a busy day for Bill Armstrong at Project Luddite, there had been many forum posts about the ARV and Biefeld-Brown effect on a forum site known as Above Top Secret as well as a site Reality Uncovered. His automated systems monitor the NSA feed for these keywords and alert his team about the activity. His team worked overtime to bury the forums in a bunch of mindless threads about the Mandela effect, water powered cars, alien abductions, the TR-3B flying triangle, and the Bob Lazar Sport Model UFO running on element 115.

His team also posted ridiculing posts to try and mock the ideas raised in the forums, that the ARV looked more like a deep sea diving bell than a spacecraft. Of course they had no real idea what a spacecraft should look like and posted a picture of the Star Trek Enterprise. They stated that no one had come forward with solid proof in the form of a peer reviewed scientific journal that the technology worked.

The goal was posting off topic posts in the offending threads as well as unhelpful or trolling posts to debunk the restricted ideas, to win the hearts and minds of the forum goers who were reading the posts and seeing an avalanche of posts debunking the forbidden technology posters. Then the team would move the restricted threads down the list in the forum as far and as fast as possible by flooding it with other posts. It was crude but it worked.

IP addresses of those talking about restricted technologies were logged and traced back to the individuals home and name and were subsequently on the monitored list. Their online habits would be monitored from that point on. No one ever got off this list. No restricted technology discussions were too unimportant in the eyes of Project Luddite. Their mission was to stay on top of discussions and deal with them before discussions turned into actions. At least for now it was all talk without concrete proof to back it up but some of the posters were calling for experiments. Such proof would never be allowed to see the light of day as long as Armstrong ran Project Luddite.

Chapter 12 – Hunt for Zero Point

I began reading a book by Nick Cook called The Hunt for Zero Point. It discussed possible Nazi research into gravity back during World War II and their program known as the Bell. It was interesting that research into forbidden technologies might have started that long ago but not too helpful in reproducing the components of the Bell. Further some believed it was merely a method to produce radioactive uranium to make a bomb as it supposedly emitted high levels of radiation making the scientists working on it deathly sick.

Nick Cook also interviewed Eugene Podkletnov in the book who stated that he had done further research into his rotating superconductor plate and when the rotational velocity was high enough, at least 25,000 rpm, the disc would lift up into the air, either its attraction to gravitational bodies reduced and/or propelled upward by some kind of force.

Then there was zero point energy, an obsession among many with somehow drawing energy from the vacuum. Many researchers in the field of free energy look to this idea to explain all sorts of different energy experiments where they claim to be getting free energy. Virtual particles continually pop into existence and then disappear again throughout the vacuum of space, throughout all of the universe. A cubic centimeter of space contains enough energy to boil the seas if it could somehow be extracted and put to use.

There is no known method to turn these virtual particles into usable energy, despite some of the cries by researchers in the field. Hal Puthoff is a preeminent scientist working on this problem though he has not had any positive results as far as we know. He has an organization that supposedly inspects experiments that defy known physics but it has seemed like more of a graveyard where these projects go to die, being delayed and receiving no funding.

However, in one of Puthoff's papers he states that the zero point field is responsible for the force of gravity and inertia. That when atoms are broken down into their constituent quarks, those quarks have a charge, either positive or negative, and the ZPF interacts with those charged quarks inside protons and neutrons. If somehow matter could be shielded from the ZPF so that the virtual particles aren't interacting with the charged quarks composing matter then matter would not be subject to the forces of gravity and inertia.

With such an effect UFO's could accelerate rapidly, make 90 degree turns and the occupants of the craft would not feel any g-forces. The lack of inertia must be part of UFO's in order to explain their ability to maneuver as they do as seen by witnesses. Occupants wouldn't get crushed by g-forces if the craft was not subject to inertia. The question is how to do it? I decided to ruminate on this subject while high off my ass on cannabis. Not too many ideas but plenty of euphoric certainty that I was again on the right track.

Chapter 13 – Heim Theory

Heim theory or Extended Heim theory is an alternative to the standard model of physics that predicts a rotating mass rotating with an outer surface speed of at least 1000m/s with a magnetic field applied perpendicular to the rotating mass of at least ten Tesla will produce a strong propulsive effect parallel to the magnetic field.

The theory hasn't been proven as creating such a powerful electromagnet and rotating disc is difficult and very expensive.

The theory also required the use of matter with odd nuclear spin. This theory could potentially explain the reason Eugene Podkletnov's rotating superconductor in a magnetic field worked. The superconductor could have been composed in part by odd nuclear spin material.

Copper, Aluminum, Bismuth, isotopes of Titanium, and other elements are all odd nuclear spin materials. Bismuth is the highest at -9/2 but it is brittle and not easily crafted into materials like spinning discs or plates. It is also far more expensive than common materials like copper and aluminum. Copper has a -3/2 nuclear spin, aluminum is 5/2. The capacitor plates in the ARV were supposedly made of copper. An odd material to use considering steel is stronger and cheaper. I think it is due to the properties of copper, it's odd nuclear spin, that is the reason that it was chosen for the capacitor plates.

This was no doubt a proof of concept vehicle. Brad Sorenson, Mark McCandlish's informant stated that the ARV looked beat up, that it had seen a lot of use. I have little doubt that subsequent versions of craft use odd nuclear spin material closer to bismuth, or maybe bismuth. If the degree of odd nuclear spin matters then bismuth might propel the craft faster than copper all things being equal. If element 115, supposedly used in the Bob Lazar Sport Model UFO, has odd nuclear spin it is possible that it is even greater than Bismuth's -9/2 odd nuclear spin.

Chapter 14 – Preparing for Doomsday

I had been amassing a movie, TV, video game, and porn collection for years now. I would rip my Netflix discs and store them on my sixteen drive 3U rackmount storage array. When I initially built the RAID 5 server (a redundant storage mechanism where the hard drives will continue working even if one stops working) it used 500GB drives, small now, (I have a RAID 1 array on my main computer that uses 4TB drives, where one hard drive mirrors the content of the other, that were purchased fairly cheaply) but at the time, top of the line, for a total storage space of 7.5TB.

I was paying about $50 a month to Netflix for the privilege of taking out eight DVDs at a time. I would go to the local Manchester library and take out the maximum of eight DVDs at a time there too. From TV series like Star Trek Voyager, Lost and the Red Green show to movies like Patriot Games and Enemy of the State. I would return the discs to Netflix and the library the next day and proceed to take out another eight discs from both organizations.

Even with the sixteen drive storage array I was rapidly filling it up and that was before Blu Ray. I had terabytes of movies, preparing for some day I didn't have an internet connection or for when Netflix Instant did not have the show or movie I wanted to see.

My video game collection consisted less of PC games though I did have a couple dozen of them, many Star Wars flight sim games like

Star Wars X-Wing Alliance, Diablo 2, Star Trek Bridge Commander, Star Trek Armada 2, Star Trek Voyager Elite Force. More than that I had thousands of ROMS for the Super Nintendo, Nintendo, Playstation, Nintendo 64, and MAME arcade emulators. A virtual treasure trove of video games, many many gigabytes of video games, far more than I would ever have time to play.

My porn collection was equally ridiculous. I cut up longer videos into the individual scenes and organized them by porn starlet with a face photo on the folder so each starlet was readily identifiable. At its max I had around five hundred folders and several hundred gigabytes of videos.

It was all a bit OCDish, a need to collect, catalog, and store all this media for some day in the future. Eventually the server did crash, even with RAID 5 being used, and I lost everything on it. But I now have Netflix and Hulu which covers a lot of shows, furthermore I don't obsessively watch the same shows over and over like I used to, I try and watch good shows that I have not seen before now. You can only laugh at the same joke or repeat the same dialogue over and over in your mind so many times before it gets old.

Chapter 15 – Nikola Tesla

Tesla was a genius, his research into the unknown produced a number of ground breaking inventions and innovations.

Tesla showed the world at the 1893 World's Expo in Chicago AC electricity, the standard used today throughout the world to send electricity from the power plants and distribute to customers at home

(Thomas Edison discovered DC electricity which does not work well over long distances nor are DC voltages easily converted from one voltage to another).

Tesla gave us the fluorescent light bulb a good 40 years before it became mainstream. He even bent the glass tubes into words effectively creating the first neon sign.

Tesla investigated electromagnetic radiation and developed X-rays, a technology we use today in hospitals to look for broken bones.

Tesla's investigations into electromagnetic radiation also resulted in his discovery of radio waves. While Guglielmo Marconi was issued the patent for the radio, years later the Supreme Court overturned the patent acknowledging that Tesla invented it first.

Tesla's forays into the radio resulted in another invention, remote control using radio waves. In 1898 he developed a model boat that was remote controlled with radio waves.

Tesla's development of AC electricity resulted in the development of electric motors using a rotating magnetic field. This invention can be seen in modern Tesla car motors, car alternators, power tools like the table saw, household appliances like blenders, and cooling fans.

Tesla's research into electromagnetic waves also resulted in the development of the laser, a device we can see in a variety of applications from laser eye surgery to DVD players.

One of Tesla's largely unknown inventions is the bifilar pancake coil. The bifilar pancake coil caught my eye as you don't hear much about it.

A standard coil of 1000 turns with 100 volts across it will have a difference of .1 volt between turns. A bifilar coil will have a difference of 50 volts between turns. This cancels out the self-inductance of the coil (a major contributor of heat). In that the stored energy is a function of the square of the voltages the energy in the bifilar coil will be 250,000 times greater than a standard coil.

Perhaps such a high amount of energy could interact with the ZPF...

Maybe I'm onto something...

Like I needed an excuse... I sparked up a bowl and got stoned pontificating about my latest detective work and what it might mean.

Chapter 16 – The Opposing Magnet, Bifilar Coil, and ARV

We know from Boyd Bushman's opposing magnet experiment that two magnets with like poles bolted together S-N-N-S reduces gravity on the magnet device in a way that two normal magnets stuck together N-S-N-S does not. In a sense a quadfilar electromagnetic coil with ground applied to the first and fourth wires and voltage applied to the second and third wires is like the Boyd Bushman magnet device.

We know there was a large multi-layer electromagnetic coil on the ARV. Rethinking the ARV's electromagnetic coil, perhaps instead of being a conventional electromagnet it is a type of multifilar electromagnetic coil, same idea as the quadfilar electromagnetic coil above just with more layers and levels. This would reduce gravity on the ARV as well as reducing inertia on the ARV if Hal Puthoff's idea on zero point energy field is real.

Perhaps the goal isn't so much to extract energy from the zero point energy field as it is to decouple the zero point energy field from the matter of the ARV. This would totally upend the traditional notion that matter can't go faster than the speed of light. If matter has no gravity or inertia then it would not take ever increasing amounts of energy to make it go faster. While no one who has looked upon the subject of the ARV and its electromagnetic coil has deduced that it is a multifilar electromagnetic coil, it seems to me to be the only possible solution.

I decided reproducing Boyd Bushman's like pole facing magnet test was a good first step in my quest for knowledge. I ordered some N42 neodymium magnets, model **RY046** with holes already in the center from **http://www.kjmagnetics.com**. I was able to find some non-magnetic brass bolts, washers, and nuts online. I made one magnet with north pole to north pole bolted together as Bushman had. The other was just two magnets magnetically attached to each other, north to south with the bolt going through it too to keep their weights the same.

I asked my brother Andrew to help me conduct this experiment by standing at the bottom of the house at the basement door as I simultaneously dropped the two objects from a second story bedroom window. After ten tests with the S-N-N-S magnet and N-S-N-S magnet, the S-N-N-S magnet device landed last every time. Boyd Bushman's experiment was confirmed, a success. I had no choice, I had to see if I could create the effect, even more powerful, with a multifilar electromagnetic coil.

Chapter 17 – Supreme Cosmic Secret

A man by the name of Gordon Novel wrote a book on the ARV and his attempts to figure out how it works and capitalize on it. Supreme Cosmic Secret can't even be found on the internet these days. I managed to find a copy buried in a directory on some site years ago. So I've got my copy, reminds me of the guy in V for Vendetta having his secret copy of the Koran.

Some of it is spot on, he too believes that the flat plate capacitors at the bottom of the craft use the Biefeld-Brown effect and states that 1,000,000 volts are dumped onto the capacitors to propel the craft. He theorizes what that effect might be including the Alcubiere warp drive idea. It is just a theory though and I cannot say what drives the Biefeld-Brown effect, what the physics are behind it.

Some of it is really out there, for example he theorizes that the ARV can travel through time. Nothing Mark McCandlish said indicated that the ARV could travel through time, there is nothing on the craft that has been identified with having time bending properties.

Bruce DePalma reported that a clock near his homopolar generator ran slower than the control clock and there was possibly a flywheel in the ARV but that would not make time travel possible. At the most it would be possible to slow the passage of time a little on board the ARV. Hardly time travel.

Some of it sets him up for ridicule like naming the capacitors on the bottom of the ARV 'flux capacitors' ripping off Back to the Future. I can see it as a joke, that he is just a fan of Back to the Future but some use it to ridicule him and everything he says.

Gordon Novel had some interesting ideas on the power source of the ARV. What if it was really just an electric motor turning a generator?

Right away any engineer will tell you that that would not work. That you can't get more energy out of the system than you put in. Gordon Novel wrote to Hal Puthoff asking him whether or not in an inertia-less environment a smaller motor could turn a bigger generator. Without inertia Puthoff said yes.

Now neither Novel nor Puthoff knew how such an inertia-less environment could be created but we do. If the generator was surrounded by a multifilar electromagnetic coil and that coil acted just like the opposing magnets it would reduce inertia on the generator allowing a small electric motor to turn a bigger generator creating overunity free energy.

Somehow the multifilar electromagnetic coil dampens the zero point energy field in its vicinity shielding the ARV from gravity and inertia and creating an inertia-less environment for the generator as well as its passengers.

It seems we now know how the ARV works, the nuts and bolts of the system: propulsion, energy, and anti-inertia. Time to get to work.

Chapter 18 – First Step: Building the Power Generator

Where do I even start?

I decided to buy an HD camera to document my experiments and which later could be distributed online to other enthusiasts and experimenters.

Somehow I need get an electric motor to turn a generator making overunity electricity.

I could use alternators. Their efficiency is poor, around 50-60% efficient, but they are cheap and flexible. An alternator can be turned into an electric motor rather easily and for far less money than a dedicated electric motor of equivalent power. Electric motors with sufficient power are not off the shelf and not cheap. With an alternator however, depending on how powerful they are, they can put out a couple horsepower.

"To eBay."

Several cheap high amperage alternators were for sale and would suit my purposes. I ordered two 250 amp alternators. That's about 3000 watts AC when run through an inverter to convert the 12volt DC to 120volt AC.

There are several ways I could connect the two alternators together. I could mount them to a board or piece of metal and use a belt. That would probably be the most reliable and conventional method of connecting the two alternators together. I could face the two alternators together and connect them with hex head sockets or nuts. I would have to glue one of the nuts on one alternator so it doesn't come off while it is rotating though since two alternators facing each other would have to spin in the same direction, the opposite that one of the alternators would normally spin which would automatically keep the nut tight.

I need to create a multifilar electromagnetic coil to wrap around the generator alternator reducing its inertia. If I used the mount alternators to a board method and used a belt I could not create an adequate coil around one of the alternators. It wouldn't full encompass the alternator.

If I mounted the alternators to end caps on a PVC tube and used the socket method I could create an excellent multifilar electromagnetic coil around the PVC.

I can't think of any other methods. I wish I could I am not crazy about either of them but good is better than perfect I guess. I ordered the 10 inch PVC end caps and PVC tube.

I took apart one of the alternators and used a 24 volt power supply to apply voltage to the 3 points in the alternator that would cause the alternator to smoothly spin along with voltage applied to the rotor to power up the spinning electromagnet. I used an Arduino along with a few other parts to control the rpm of the alternator motor. It should now be sufficient to spin the alternator generator

Mounting the alternator to the end cap was easy. The alternator had 4 bolts that ran the length of the alternator and they were hex heads which unscrewed from the back. I had to order and use some longer bolts than the ones that came in the alternator but this method of attaching the alternators to the PVC end caps worked fine.

Connecting the double ended hex socket however was not easy. I had to cut the PVC pipe smaller and smaller so the double ended socket would reach. Lining up the two hex nuts on the alternators was tricky but with some finagling I managed to do it.

Now I had to create the multifilar coil. The ARV used 1/4" copper wire rod with approximately 1/4" of dielectric surrounding the copper rod. There was no information on the voltage levels that went through the ARV's electromagnetic coil. At a maximum it could have been about 125,000 volts. There is no way I could replicate the copper rod multifilar coil, especially if the voltage was that high. I would have to find 1/4" copper rod, find a way of bending it precisely so that there was always a 1/4" space on all sides of the copper rod, then encompass the copper rod with epoxy to prevent arcing between the coils of copper rod. Obviously I have no means of creating that copper rod coil.

I could use conventional wire but it would require many many windings to create a multifilar coil that encompasses the alternator generator. This method would allow me to run high voltages through the coil depending on the dielectric strength of the coating of the wire. The higher the dielectric strength of the wire coating, the higher the voltage that can be run through the wire.

Spark! I just had an idea. Why not use computer ribbon cable?

The voltages are limited to 300 volts in most ribbon cables but you can buy ribbon cable 80 wires wide. I am not great or even good at math and physics equations. Plus I am not sure equations to do what I was doing existed. What would create a more powerful effect, less turns of wire at a high voltage like the 30kV a flyback transformer would put out or more turns of wire at a voltage of 300V. Using the 80 wide ribbon cable was easier so I decided to use that for my overunity free energy generator experiment.

Unfortunately there is no formula I know of to predict how many turns of the 80 wire wide cable are needed so I decided to use the whole spool. I have three 80 wire wide ribbon cables spools side by side wrapped around the PVC pipe that encompasses the alternator generator. The start of wire 1 is connected to the end of wire 2, the start of wire 2 is connected to 0 volts, and the end of wire 1 is connected to 300 volts. The rest of the wires are connected in kind.

I took to eBay again to find a 300 voltage power supply. With a multifilar coil there is no net magnetic field so the power comes from the difference in voltage between adjacent wires not the current going through the wires. As a result I didn't need a lot of current going through the coil once it was energized and as we know a standard multifilar electromagnetic coil has 250,000 times the energy of a traditional electromagnetic coil using the same length of wire.

I took to eBay to find a 3000 watt inverter to change the electricity from the alternator generator's 12 volts DC to 120 volts AC. I then connected a powerful UPS to the inverter to give a battery powered buffer in case there are dips in the alternator generators output. I also connected the 300 volt power supply to the UPS. Finally I connected the power supply powering the alternator motor to the UPS as well.

Everything that required electricity was now powered by the battery backup UPS. This would provide a few minutes of run time if the alternator generator isn't putting out enough electricity to feed the inverter.

I plugged in several computers, monitors, mini-fridges, air conditioners to the UPS and it purred like a kitten. I was getting about 1500 watts output from the contraption of parts, free and clear! It works!!

I couldn't stop there, I would have to try using the 30kV wire and 150kV wire I found on eBay. It's possible that they will reduce inertia on the alternator generator even more and I will be able to use less electricity to power the alternator motor getting out more watts, maybe 2000 or 2500 watts if I am lucky.

I made sure to film the contraption running for half an hour showing that nothing was plugged into the wall, following the cables so viewers could see how everything was hooked up and that there were no tricks.

Chapter 19 – Increase in Traffic related to the Alien Reproduction Vehicle

Director Armstrong was unnerved, his division heads told him that there has been an increase in talk and speculation about the Alien Reproduction Vehicle in forums across the internet, from abovetopsecret.com, one of their honey pots, to realityuncovered.com another one of their honey pots.

The speculation was very close to the mark on forbidden propulsion technologies including the Biefeld-Brown effect, Heim theory which predicted the propulsion effects seen in Eugene Podkletnov's rotating superconductor though even regular conductors with odd nuclear spin would work according to Heim theory. The authors were calling for people to conduct experiments, and some said they would, to see if there was anything to these supposed effects despite the ridiculing of the forum trolls on the payroll of Project Luddite.

Fortunately for Director Armstrong the principle authors were not connected through TOR so Project Luddite was able to decipher who the authors were, where the authors came from, their IP addresses, email accounts, cellphone numbers, their physical addresses. There were weaknesses in the TOR network, about 5% of users at any one time could be identified due to compromised TOR entrance and exit nodes. The TOR browser specifically has a weakness but it required the user to enable JavaScript.

The forum authors' user names would be followed from now on, Armstrong hoped they would not actually conduct experiments because he might have to have them killed depending on what they accomplish.

Either way Director Armstrong decided he would alert his division heads at Project Luddite that some targets might be experimenting with creating forbidden propulsion technologies and that in depth surveillance, remotely turning on their computer webcams and microphones, and cellphone microphones, of the targets would be needed to stay on top of anything and everything they might do.

Project Luddite's supporters in Congress, the elite of the Democrat and Republican parties, have been lobbying for mass surveillance and putting backdoors in encryption technology to their fellow party members in an effort to deanonymize everyone and to keep these forbidden technologies hidden and those looking into them monitored and killed if necessary. Edward Snowden's NSA leak had thrown a monkey wrench into their machinations thanks to his exposure of the wide spread surveillance of all the peoples of the world currently going on in the Five Eyes nations: United States, Great Britain, Canada, Australia, and New Zealand.

This kind of monitoring had been suspected of going on for decades with the Five Eyes Echelon system but no one on the inside had revealed just how extensive that spying was until Snowden. It had been said that all phone calls, all faxes were collected by the echelon system, being before the modern internet.

There is no reason to believe they haven't advanced their capabilities with the development of the internet to match the ones they had pre-internet.

Chapter 20 – Dinner with Steve

It was just an ordinary day. I was on the forums arguing with other members on the merits of the Alien Reproduction Vehicle, its propulsion systems, theories on how it worked, what have you. A typical day for me lately, as obsessed as I was about the ARV. The rest of my life just didn't have a hold of my attention like the ARV. I was obsessed with it, I couldn't put it out of my mind. Where there is smoke there is fire and I was sure the ARV was a raging four alarm fire of an inferno.

My friend Steve called me at the last minute about meeting him at Pepe's for a beer after work but I didn't have anything to do, taking a break even a brief one was good with me. Plus I could let him in on the latest information I had discovered and hear the latest happenings at his place of employment. I arrived at Pepe's to find a suspicious looking man standing by the door to the rear entrance of the restaurant. As I walked past him and inside the restaurant he followed me in and went to two of his associates.

A waitress came by me and whispered, "this is just for show" and proceeded to welcome them loudly to the establishment, that it was good to see them again. I was getting more paranoid by the minute.

I got a chilling feeling that these people were there for me. I stated to Steve that I decided I was not gonna work on the project anymore, that the government would squash me like a bug. One of the men stated to his friends, "see nothing to worry about". I lied stating I was gonna work on a tricorder. As the men left, the one that had stood by the entrance says to me "this is the third time we have been watching you".

I knew I was in deep, I wanted to continue my research and I had to find help before they decided it was just in their interest to kill me.

I decided I would need to find some allies, I hoped there were people from Wikileaks in the bar and I was about to go down the rabbit hole but sadly there was not. I needed to hit up IRC channels and look for members of 2600. I had subscribed to their quarterly magazine for several years, bought a hat that I wore throughout college, and listened to their weekly radio program. If any group could help me it was them.

Chapter 21 – Building the Marx Generator Voltage Multiplier for the Brown Capacitors

While I stated to Steve and for the men to hear me that I was done with the project I just couldn't let it go. I was too emotionally invested in the project, I was too obsessed with it. I proceeded with my plan and started work on the voltage multiplier.

Since the best method for propelling the flat parallel plate capacitors was pulsed high voltages that ruled out a steady DC output of a Cockcroft Walton generator. Perhaps with a rotating system like a distributor cap a Cockcroft Walton generator could be used applying voltages to all the plates as it spun around but that would be a complicated part to build and moving parts are the enemy of reliability, never mind custom made moving parts. The Marx generator would be the best method of producing high voltage pulses, it is solid state, no moving parts, definitely the way to make longest lasting components.

A Marx generator is a form of voltage multiplier. It shares many commonalities with a Cockcroft Walton generator, also a voltage multiplier. While a CW voltage multiplier outputs steady DC, a Marx voltage multiplier outputs pulsed DC. A CW voltage multiplier uses AC input while a Marx needs an input of DC current. Voltage multipliers consist of stages. In each stage in both voltage multipliers there is a capacitor. The capacitors charge up in parallel meaning each capacitor takes in the base input voltage applied at the very first stage. When the capacitors discharge they do so in series, voltage adding to voltage up through the stages, depending the number of stages, creating a much higher voltage than the input. In a Cockcroft Walton generator diodes direct the electricity up through the stages. In a Marx generator each stage has a spark gap that the electricity jumps across as the electricity goes up through the stages, this is why the DC current has a pulsed output. The materials used in the spark gap have to be resistant to heat or they will degrade quickly especially at high voltages. Tungsten is an excellent material for use in spark gaps as it has a very high melting temperature.

A Marx generator can make use of simple regular spark gaps but in order to really increase control and the frequency, the number of pulses per second, a trigatron would have to be used at the first stage. A trigatron would take the place of the first spark gap in the first stage of the Marx generator. With such a setup and a powerful enough power supply feeding the Marx generator the trigatron can be activated a hundred times a second leading the Marx generator to output a hundred pulses a second.

To reduce the number of stages in the Marx generator while outputting 1Megavolt the input of DC current into the Marx generator should have as high a voltage as possible. Flyback transformers, a device with a primary coil that electricity runs through whose energy is passed magnetically to the secondary coil which raises the voltage, can be found in CRT monitors and CRT televisions. However those devices have all but disappeared. Furthermore most flybacks have a diode, a little gate, turning the natural AC output of the flyback into DC. Those diodes can overheat and die with heavy usage and they are impossible to fix. As stated earlier, we do need DC current into a Marx generator so a diode has to be used to filter the output of the flyback transformers.

I hit up some experts on the forum at **4hv.org** a high voltage site with many experts on building Tesla coils and voltage multipliers. After posting that I was looking for some AC input AC output flybacks, I got a response. The member knew some people in China who could make the flybacks for me for a low price and ship them to America. I couldn't hide behind anonymity or encryption for this one. I had to keep my TOR identities I had started using separate from my regular non-anonymous persona. So I used my real name and PayPal to pay the Chinese vendor and in a few weeks I was looking at four 200 watt 30kV flyback transformers.

I considered using AC output flybacks to drive the first stage of a Cockcroft Walton generator. This would double the voltage of the flybacks and output DC current. The downside is since the flyback outputted 30kV, a Cockcroft Walton generator would double that to 60kV and I would need to find 60kV capacitors for the rest of the stages of the Marx generator. Those are far and away more expensive than 30kV capacitors and have much larger energy storage potential which means they take longer to fully charge which means it would take longer to discharge decreasing the pulse rate into the Brown capacitors. So either I double the voltage going into the Marx generator or I double the stages in the Marx generator to get the 1 Megavolt output. I opted for double the stages.

There was another problem to deal with. In a Marx generator solidly on terra firma I could connect the ground of the Marx generator to a spike driven into the ground. However if it was off the ground I would have no ground to connect the Marx generator to. I decided to use an idea I caught on site about building Marx generators. They have one Marx generator creating a positive voltage and the other creates an identical negative voltage. This way I could connect the positive lead off the Brown capacitor to the positive lead on the Marx generator and the grounding lead off the Brown capacitor to the negative lead on the second Marx generator.

I ran the flybacks in parallel giving me 800 watts of power flowing into the two Marx generators at 30kV.

Luckily there are some calculators on the web to tell you how many stages you need with a given input voltage and a desired output voltage.

Building the Marx generators phases was tricky. I had to use capacitors rated to at least 30kV though I aimed for 40kV to give some head room. Unfortunately I could not find any cheap 40kV ceramic capacitors on eBay. The highest voltage ratings I could find for cheap ceramic capacitors was 30kV. That would be pushing the reliability of the capacitors, I just hoped they would hold.

I also used low energy storage capacitors, ceramics with only a few picofarads of power. This way they could be charged faster and the faster the capacitors are charged in the Marx generator, the faster it can pulse out DC current. Instead of using resistors I went with inductors as they waste less of the power going through the generator and they allow for faster charging and spark rates.

Manually grinding the end of the tungsten rods into spheres was a slow tedious process but to reduce waste heat and leaking electricity into the air, corona, rounded spark gaps were a must.

I also put clear flexible plastic tubes creating a tunnel between the spark gaps. This would reduce the chance of a short circuit in the Marx generator. Creating this tunnel would allow me to immerse the Marx generator in transformer oil, or for a more permanent solution, epoxy, without putting anything but air between the spark gaps. Coating all wires, inductors, and capacitors would definitely reduce the chance of a short circuit or electricity flowing where it's not supposed to.

Chapter 22 – Biefeld-Brown Parallel Plate Capacitor

Building the capacitor would be problematic. The higher the voltage the easier it can arc through a material and I was looking to put 1 Megavolt, 1,000,000 volts, pulsed into the capacitor. I found the sheets of copper ½ inch thick online easily and for a reasonable price. I decided to use two one foot by one foot square plates, one positive the other negative.

The dielectric, the material between the plates that has to be capable of keeping the electricity from arcing through, finding that, was quite difficult. I wanted to find material with the highest dielectric strength as possible. This would allow me to make the capacitor's dielectric as thin as possible which also increases the energy storage capacity of the capacitor.

I could order some solid materials like Teflon or other synthetic plastics. In Gordon Novel's Supreme Cosmic Secret the material G10 was hypothesized to be the material between the plates. It has a very high dielectric strength, resistance of electricity to flow through it, and it is fireproof.

That alone would not be enough to make the Biefeld-Brown capacitor. There would be air bubbles between the copper plates and G10 which would be a starting point for the electricity to arc through. I needed to use an epoxy, an epoxy with a very high dielectric strength and make a sandwich with the bottom copper plate, a thin layer of epoxy, the G10 dielectric, a thin layer of epoxy, and the top copper plate.

A site called **http://www.matweb.com**provides all sorts of detailed information on a wide variety of materials. I used this to find a clear epoxy with very high dielectric strength to use in the capacitors. To get the bubbles out of the epoxy I needed to put the epoxy in a vacuum. I used a vacuum chamber and air conditioning coolant vacuum pump to suck out the air in the chamber. This causes the tiny gas bubbles in the epoxy to rise to the surface and leave the epoxy, making the epoxy electrically stronger than it would be if never placed in a vacuum.

Furthermore to prevent arcing out the sides or top and bottom of the capacitor it needed to be fully encased. I added a sheet of G10 to the top and bottom of the capacitor with a thin layer of epoxy in between the top and bottom copper plates and the top and bottom G10 sheets. So essentially the makeup of the capacitor was G10-Epoxy-Copper Plate-Epoxy-G10-Epoxy-Copper Plate-Epoxy-G10. To prevent arcing out the sides of the capacitor I used epoxy, thick enough to prevent any arcing. I created a form and poured in the epoxy providing a thick layer on all sides of the capacitor.

I had two wires coming off the capacitor, one to each copper plate. They would be connected to the Marx generators positive and negative poles and encased in epoxy as well.

This item is the meat and potatoes of the whole experiment. I could reduce gravity and inertia's hold on a craft as much as I'd like but without a propulsive element the goal of having a flying car that can take off and land vertically or a spacecraft propelled without a propellant is gone. Luckily I think all that smoke, the ARV, the study with low pulsed voltages, the study with a moderate steady voltage, leads to a definite fire. I was certain of it. As a good scientist that should not be the case, but I wasn't a good scientist, I was a detective, and the evidence to date had stacked up pretty well in my opinion.

Chapter 23 – Wolfpack Hockey Against the Glass

My brother Andrew had gotten hockey tickets to a minor league Wolfpack hockey game in the Hartford CT Civic Center. We went with one of his friends from work, his girlfriend, Dustin, and Gary. I didn't really follow the team but that didn't mean I couldn't have a good time.

Hockey is a fast paced game, its not like baseball, turnovers happen constantly with some breakaway shots on goal. You've also got penalties leaving a team down a man on the ice. That really creates greater scoring opportunities and increases the pace of the game. The tickets were great, front row, right against the glass or plastic or whatever they use.

I wasn't going to let $8.00 beers at the concession stands prevent me from getting drunk. I smuggled in a flask full of Jim Beam bourbon whiskey. I had gotten the flask as a birthday present from my friend Mike who knew I liked whiskey. I took that flask with me everywhere from restaurants and bars to be able to get a buzz without racking up a large alcohol bill, to parties where is it was BYOB. I bought a large bottle of lemonade from the concession stands. I drank some of the lemonade and emptied my flask into the lemonade bottle.

Over the course of the night I got feisty jeering the players of the other team, a few 'you suck #XX', trying to distract the opposing team and help the Wolfpack get a victory. I was pretty inebriated, my flask held eight shots of the Jim Beam whiskey and I drank it all, but thankfully I was not driving.

It was a good time, another good night. I can't remember if the Wolfpack won or lost, I think they won, but it didn't affect my enjoyment of the game or my time with my friends.

Chapter 24 – Putting the Prototype Together

I wasn't willing to fire up the Biefeld-Brown flat parallel plate capacitor at home for I had heard rumors that the U.S. government had satellites in orbit that could detect their energy signature, the particles the device releases. For example there was a friend of a scientist that Mark McCandlish mentions in his interview who stated that the scientist was attempting to test the dielectric strength of a material and created a flat parallel plate capacitor with the material between it. While putting in half a million to a million volts the capacitor levitated. Somehow his university project was quickly discovered by some sort of government group, his experiment taken, and orders given to him and his associates familiar with his discovery to keep their mouths shut about it.

With the energy generator there was no particles or energy being given off, the zero point energy field was being dampened by the coil but not generating any exotic particles that the capacitor would. Even that was a guess though, satellites can detect variations in gravity in different areas of the world. It's possible they could do the same with the zero point energy field.

It was a risk powering up the capacitor at all, who knows what detection abilities the government might have, satellite coverage over all the planet, or at least all the U.S., but I was willing to risk it. I had to, or I would never know if it worked or not.

I drove around till I found a wide open field far from my home. I had taken my emergency cellphone out of the truck and left it at home. I didn't want the government tracking me to the field with my cellphone signal while the prototype was running, that would be a major rookie mistake, bush league.

I tried to keep as much of the device in my truck bed so after the experiment I could pack up and get the hell out of there, hopefully before anyone notices me. I moved the Marx generator off the truck, it being connected to my UPS which was powered by my overunity alternator generator.

I moved the Brown capacitor off the truck as well, who knows what might happen when electricity was applied. I thought I had gotten rid of all the air bubbles but who knows, there could still be weak spots in the dielectric and the last thing I wanted to do was fry my truck leaving me stranded in the field just after powering up the capacitor.

I set the pulse rate of the Marx generator to one hundred pulses per second. That was about the maximum pulse rate the Marx generator could charge up and discharge into the Brown capacitor.

I am reminded of a saying by Capt Benjamin Sisko, to paraphrase it: "All I have to do is throw the switch, either it will work or it won't. Worrying about it won't change anything."

I flipped the switch and the capacitor shot into the sky ripping out the cables attached to the Marx generator.

"Yahhhooooo... I knew it would work, I just knew it!!"

The capacitor came down with a loud thump. It looked intact, just the connecting wires had been damaged. That was enough for me, I threw the Marx generator and the Brown capacitor into the truck bed and got the hell out of there. I wasn't taking any chances that my experiment might be detected and traced back to me, the longer I was there the higher the likelihood I'd be caught.

I had one goal in mind now, to create my own flying car and show it to the world, to make sure anyone and everyone knew about it.

Chapter 25 – Biefeld-Brown Capacitor Anomaly Detected

Project Luddite was in a tizzy. A Biefeld-Brown flat parallel plate capacitor anomaly had been detected by the Homeworld Security satellite network in orbit and appeared to originate in an open field in Connecticut. It definitely wasn't any of their own craft, their positions and movements had all been accounted for. There were no houses or buildings in the area.

Armstrong had his subordinates check the NSA feed again, see if anyone was claiming responsibility for the anomaly, bragging or otherwise talking about the forbidden technology in any capacity. So far they had no leads and this did not sit well with Armstrong. His whole job was to keep forbidden technologies from becoming public knowledge and now someone had gone past talking about it, hypothesizing about it, to actually building it, and proving to him or herself that such a technology did exist.

Unfortunately luck was not with Project Luddite, there was no satellite video coverage over the field at the time so they could not see what had happened, who was there, how they got there, where they had been and where they were going.

Homeworld Security's satellites would be on high alert for even the tiniest Brown capacitor anomaly, the men of these unacknowledged SAPs (special access programs) were determined to confiscate the technology immediately and make the experimenter an offer he or she could not refuse.

Chapter 26 – Throwing My Hat Over the Wall

Kevin Smith made a bunch of good movies and I will admit to dressing up as Bluntman for several Halloweens, for one I was Bob, I was often silent, up in my head, I could grow a beard, and I liked cannabis.

Anyway Smith did a short comedy video featuring his titular characters Dante and Randal from his cult classic Clerks. In it Randal describes his displeasure at being stuck in traffic and that we did not have any flying cars like he had been promised by cartoons like the Jetsons so many years ago. Randal believed someone somewhere had to be working on the flying car, that someone had thrown their hat over the wall for the good of mankind, committed to doing it.

I did not have an engineering degree, I did not have any vocational experience in welding, limited computer programming experience, all I had was the mindset of a detective, and an obsession to build the flying car. I was throwing my hat over the wall to build the flying car.

But before I could build it I needed to design it. I could learn CAD (Computer Aided Drafting), it would be beneficial to create a real blueprint in CAD rather than relying on pencil, paper, ruler, and compass.

A few sketches on paper to get an idea would help though.

The craft needed VTOL (vertical take off and landing) capability. No runways, no helipads, the ability to precisely land in a parking space while flying. This would require a sophisticated sensor suite not unlike the backup cameras and parallel parking technology present in some new cars. The craft would also need to be able to stably hover, to stay in one spot when the throttle was at zero and the flight stick was in neutral.

I had to be able to control the thrust the Brown capacitors were capable of. I can't jump from 0-1000mph in one second when I tap on the gas pedal. Even with a multifilar coil surrounding the circumference of the craft, dampening the zero point field and reducing inertia in the craft, I needed precise control of movement if I were to be flying around. I needed precise control of the acceleration caused by the Brown capacitors. I had to regulate the pulses of voltage into the capacitors, increasing and decreasing the firing frequency of the Marx generators as needed.

I had read in McCandlish's interview that the ARV could go past the speed of light. For a flying car that was definite overkill. I wanted a flying craft that could get anywhere in the world in under an hour. This would revolutionize the notion of borders turning the globe into one big city. Go shopping for groceries in the third world to pay less and help out poor farmers. Have french pastries for breakfast in Paris, a t-bone steak in Austin, Texas for lunch, and fresh sushi in Okinawa, Japan for dinner. A true global village.

I decided on a triangular shape for the design that would fly and land like Boba Fett's ship Slave 1 in Star Wars.

Two Brown capacitors in each corner, one on the top of the craft to propel forward, the other on the bottom of the craft to propel backward. Each capacitor would have its own set of Marx generators as I could not come up with an easy way to switch the electricity between plates. Any switch I could think of would arc over rendering the switch useless.

I would use three overunity free energy alternator generator devices on the sides of the triangle to provide sufficient power to the Marx generators as well as the on-board flight computer, GPS, and array of Raspberry Pi and Arduino sensor controllers.

I wanted the skin of the craft to be lightweight, I could use fiberglass or carbon fiber, not exactly cheap but strong but not easier to work with than sheet metal for a novice like me. I didn't need a glass canopy, I would be using video cameras to provide a feed to my on-board monitors. It would give me versatility in being able to see in any direction I had cameras. According to Mark McCandlish the paint on the ARV looked brushed on with flecks of lead. Probably to reduce any residual radiation in the cockpit either from the ARV or from radiation in space.

I would need large foam blocks to create molds for the skin material if I used carbon fiber or fiberglass.

On the other hand using nothing fancy, mostly flat plates I could use cheap thin aluminum sheets for the skin and paint it flat black with lead flecks in it.

I also wanted mounting brackets on the three corners of the ARV but more on that later.

I decided on a single seater cockpit, It would be nice to be able to take someone up in it given the opportunity but it is very much a prototype and I wouldn't want the responsibility if the vehicle's systems fail and the flying car crashed.

Somehow I would need to convert the analog flight stick and throttle control into a series of pulses into the appropriate capacitors. I could interface the flight controls with an ardunio and then connect the sensor ports on the Arduino to the the Marx generators trigatrons.

Or I could use a regular keyboard and mouse and attempt to create an LCARS Star Trek TNG type vehicle control, something along the lines of controls in the Bridge Commander video game. Something to think about.

First things first, I need to build ten 1 Megavolt Marx generators, one for each capacitor.

I need to build five 1 Megavolt capacitors.

I need to build two prototype overunity alternator generators based on the higher voltage wiring. Then I would need to pick the best one and use that in my flying car.

I need to build an Arduino controller to control the pulsing rate of the various Marx generators depending on maneuvering and throttle.

I need to use a mapping software that I can use my flight controls to aim at the destination and run it on autopilot.

Clearly, a lot of planning and work is required.

Chapter 27 – Homeworld Security

Homeworld Security ran many different activities in their duty to protect the planet from destruction due to human, alien, or robotic threats.

Back in the 50's Eisenhower met with a group of aliens known as the Greys. There had been and continues to be a working relationship with their people.

Part of the agreement was helping us, at the time, just the U.S. but now Russia, China, Great Britain, and France, the permanent members of the U.N. Security Council, to construct a planetary defense system to repel any serious threats as well as set up a system to allow the coming and going of alien species to earth.

All this was kept secret from the public as it was felt we were not ready and that top shelf alien technology would put domestic businesses out of business. A cynical perspective would say that people are dying while the technology to save them goes unused. Homeworld Security furiously gathered all the alien technologies that they could find for their own purposes.

They already possessed some interstellar starships capable of faster than light propulsion as well as defensive and offensive systems. Shields, armor plating, laser beams, plasma beams, teleportation, replicators, Biefeld-Brown flat parallel plate capacitor propulsion, anti-gravity and anti-inertia technology, wormhole technology, Homeworld Security had just finished construction on their flagship packed to the gills with these advanced technologies.

They already had mining operations on the rare earth metals asteroids in the asteroid belt between Mars and Jupiter.

And now a potential wrinkle in their operation, a gravitational anomaly in the middle of a field in Connecticut. So far they had no definite leads, many individuals had been making numerous posts on forums across the internet about the Alien Reproduction Vehicle and the theories on how it was propelled but that was a far cry from building something. Even so it was a good place to start.

Project Luddite had been created by Homeworld Security to prevent this exact thing. There was no telling with social media as popular as it is and an internet that, outside of China and North Korea, was largely censorship free, the kind of damage that could be done if information on a successful test of the technology went viral.

Tracking down the perpetrator(s) was Project Luddite's job and they were good at it. Homeworld Security had bigger things on their plate.

One such concern was North Korea. They had just detonated a nuclear bomb in another test and they were continuing to work on their albeit poor, long range missile technology. Even China their supposed ally was really just a system of control along with the UN to keep North Korea contained.

But the politicians, the Gang of Eight, who oversaw Homeworld Security and Project Luddite in Congress were chomping at the bit to use the advanced alien technologies to press a confrontation with North Korea, decimating their military and nuclear program. The President and U.S. military was more cautious though, all it would take was a nuclear weapon smuggled across the DMZ and South Korea might never recover, millions could die.

If Project Luddite failed it could force a confrontation between Homeworld Security and North Korea. North Korea would not be allowed to develop forbidden propulsion technologies that would allow them to deliver nukes anywhere in the world. This might be overstating the threat as MAD (Mutually Assured Destruction) was still a political reality and would likely keep North Korea in check regardless of the success or failure of Project Luddite.

Chapter 28 – Chinese Espionage

A Chinese military officer by the name of Lu Su arrived at the Shanghai Airport preparing to board a flight to North Korea under the guise of meeting with their military leadership to discuss defensive technologies the Chinese were considering selling to North Korea in exchange for natural resources like coal, one of North Korea's biggest exports to China.

In reality Lu Su had stolen information from Chinese intelligence's Homeworld Security division about Biefeld-Brown flat parallel plate capacitor propellantless propulsion, the forbidden technology Thomas Townsend Brown had discovered nearly a century ago. Lu Su was planning on giving the technology to the North Koreans so they could finally build working ICBMs that would reach the U.S.

Lu Su felt a confrontation was coming, a power struggle, between the U.S. and China. Not just cause of the U.S.'s disputes with China in the South China Seas but a power struggle over who would be the future superpower of the world. He felt working with the U.S. to control the world was a mistake and that only a China led world would bring true honor and prosperity to his homeland and his people. By giving the North Koreans the forbidden propulsion technology they could be used as a proxy force to attack the U.S. without China feeling the brunt of any retaliation, especially considering Lu Su was acting alone without his government's permission.

Lu Su was hoping to change the balance of power in the world with his actions, to create a rogue nuclear power that would attack and decimate China's enemies. It did not even require a nuclear detonation in one of America's cities, a high altitude detonation of a nuclear weapon would emit an electromagnetic pulse frying all electronics: computers, cellphones, ISPs, cable companies, cars, power plants across the U.S. With the Brown capacitor technology North Korea's ICBMs would be able to reach that altitude over the

U.S., to detonate one of their nukes where it would do the most electrical damage.

Lu Su's passport was in order and he proceeded to board his flight.

Chapter 29 – The Torrent Gambit

With my documentary complete I had to get it out to as many eyes and ears as possible. A normal post to Youtube wouldn't cut it. The thing with Google is that a lot of people have to link to your content for it to show up well in its search engine listings. With Youtube a person has to be searching for what you posted or your video has to get lots and lots of views to appear on the front page. Without that your video can remained buried under an avalanche of other videos and web pages.

I got to thinking about torrents. By itself it is no better a distribution for this documentary than Youtube or Google. But, I could name my torrents popular movies and television shows like a Game of Thrones, Mr Robot, or Captain American Civil War. These fake torrents would get downloaded and people would see the documentary. Sure they might not watch it but with a catchy intro that pulls in the viewer I am sure I could get a bunch of people hooked into watching the whole thing and redistributing the torrents to other people as well.

This would have to be precisely timed with my vehicle launch so that if the authorities catch on to what I am doing with the torrents they would be unable to get to me and stop my vehicle launch in time. To succeed the government has to not be able to put the genie back in the bottle.

I would also use a torrent with my real documentary's name: Forbidden Technology - Propellantless Propulsion, Anti-Gravity, Anti-Inertia, and Overunity Free Energy Revealed. As it spreads more and more users would upload my torrent to others and if I'm lucky it becomes popular enough to reach the front page of torrent sites and catches on like wildfire.

One other avenue of getting the word out is spam email. People hate getting spam but it persists because it is effective, the companies selling products over it get a return on their investment that is worth the cost of mass emailing millions of people. I could take advantage of this reality.

I could create an ebook from my documentary and find the largest email list on the internet, hire a spammer company, and send out my ebook to everyone on the list. Again not everyone would read it but enough people would assuming the government did not have the ability to analyze and intercept email messages on a global scale, hopefully the government would be unable to get the toothpaste back in the tube which is my primary goal.

Chapter 30 – The World's Biggest Publicity Stunt

Torrents of my documentary and ebooks spammed to everyone would hopefully be enough, at least I'd like to think. But I don't think that would be enough, I would need a massive publicity stunt on live TV to really blow the lid off of things. I considered flying my craft over the Times Square ball drop in New York City during the New Years Eve celebration and announcing my message about forbidden technology there.

I could think of only one thing that would make the maximum impact I wanted.

Landing my craft at the 50 yard line of the Super Bowl. I could mount bullhorns to each corner of the craft to send out a prerecorded message telling the people in the stands and the world of the technology. It is unlikely the TV producers would cut the feed as the craft landed on the field. It would be too much of a shock and if I am lucky, government does not have control over the TV feed.

The Super Bowl is the single most watched event on TV during the year, even more so than New Years Eve celebrations. Millions upon millions would watch it and see my short speech and reference to the documentary torrent on the internet.

The only issues I see are that the Super Bowl has to be at a stadium with an open roof. A closed stadium would not work. And any anti-aircraft weaponry the military might have around the stadium would have to not be used. Hopefully they would not be willing to blow up an aircraft over a stadium risking the fallout killing people and doing it during the biggest TV event of the year.

I tend to think those wielding the cameras during the Super Bowl would be in too much shock to cut away or go to commercial, especially if the sight of the craft made them think it was extraterrestrial.

Chapter 31 – Project All Seeing Eye

Project Luddite was good at their job, that much Bill Armstrong knew. But there were clues that slipped through even their fingers never mind the pantheon of actual crimes that the rest of the NSA was attempting to watch and stop. Bill Armstrong and his team were tasked by Homeworld Security to develop an AI, Project All Seeing Eye, that would replace the NSA's current monitoring technology, one that could find those clues, put the flimsy pieces of evidence together to ferret out targets and criminals.

Project All Seeing Eye would not just document people's internet and communications technologies but their purchases, their movements, their vocal patterns, their heat signatures. Any type of information related to a person would be cataloged and patterns discovered.

Bill Armstrong and his team were developing the next generation Project Luddite, a system so comprehensive that data centers were being built near hydroelectric dams and nuclear plants to get enough energy to power the new computer systems.

Soon, very soon, All Seeing Eye would have access to all public cameras, public microphones, private security feeds, private webcams on people's home computers, cellphone microphones and cameras, cloud storage systems, and personal computers.

Bill Armstrong was developing All Seeing Eye to install its core code in every private computers' firmware: motherboard bios, hard drive firmware, video card bios, network card firmware, everything. From there it could communicate directly with All Seeing Eye's mainframes bypassing the OS and any firewalls on the OS. Modern motherboard bios, hard drive firmware, video card bios, network card firmware, USB memory stick firmware, SD card firmware, are not scanned by antivirus scanners and not detectable. Formatting the hard drive and reinstalling the operating system would be useless, it would not remove the core code once installed on the firmware of the system. Once a system was compromised it was owned forever.

That was just a start, its backdoors would soon be in every commercial router and hardware firewall allowing All Seeing Eye's mainframes to communicate with its compromised systems without the traffic appearing in router and firewall logs.

All Seeing Eye would actively attempt and if Bill Armstrong did his job right install its core code on all electronic communications systems everywhere. The only possible way to evade it would be to have an air-gaped system. But to put and take information onto such systems storage media would have to be used and they would be compromised.

But All Seeing Eye was not just tasked with monitoring everything, it was a true artificial intelligence designed to detect and decipher the everyday actions of everyone.

Go to Home Depot and pay cash for that grow light and fertilizer, All Seeing Eye would recognize your facial features in the security camera feed, your voice when you were asking an employee for the lighting aisle number and record your purchases in its database alerting the DEA in your area that you are growing plants in your home, could be cannabis.

There would be nothing All Seeing Eye could not see, no behavior that would go undetected, no premeditated action it would not recognize.

The Gang of Eight who had been pressing for it and were the only ones in Congress to know about it stated they wanted to end terrorism with this new weapon. But function creep was inevitable not to mention that it would be a complete violation of the 4th Amendment. The NSA's spying powers had already been used to go after drug traffickers and users and there is no reason to believe those spying powers wouldn't continue to be used with renewed vigor with the launch of All Seeing Eye.

It was a mission Bill Armstrong and his team believed in, if you have nothing to hide you have nothing to fear.

It was Bill's hope that with All Seeing Eye they could identify the person behind the gravitational anomaly in Connecticut. Present monitoring technology had not been able to put together a profile of items that had to be purchased and who purchased them, in order to craft such a device. The system just did not have enough access to company databases, sales records. All Seeing Eye, he hoped, would be able to spot the required purchases, who purchased them according to retailers compromised databases, and put together the identity of the culprit.

Chapter 32 – The Overrated Risk of Terrorism

Terrorism is a very touchy subject with very strong opinions on all sides. There are emotional, rational, and wise views on the problem of terrorism.

The emotional argument against terrorism often views an all in approach where we stop at absolutely nothing to end terrorism in the United States and our world. This view can be formed by those whom terrorism directly hurt, those who lost family, friends, coworkers, and neighbors as well as those who fear losing those close to them.

Terrorism is a risk that could happen at any time, any place, to any person, for any reason or no reason at all. It isn't a force of nature, it is other humans murdering other humans. That is something as a society we cannot tolerate.

Then there is the rational view on the problem of terrorism. Terrorism is extraordinarily rare and kills a very small number of people. Car accidents claim over 30,000 lives each year in the United States alone. The flu claims the lives of approximately 25,000 people every year in the U.S. The money we spend on eliminating these deaths pales in comparison to what we spend on fighting terrorism. It doesn't make any sense. If we looked at the issue rationally we would vaccinate everyone who wanted one against the flu every flu season required to be covered by every health insurance company, medicare, and medicaid for free, even paid by the taxpayer if necessary.

If we are willing to spend tremendous amounts of money fighting terrorism then we should spend that much more vaccinating people against the flu.

We should also be pressing full steam ahead on self-driving cars and self-flying cars, creating a safe transportation system where computers control cars eliminating car crashes due to all sorts of reasons and enable those who cannot drive to still have transportation.

The rational position would be to spend our finite budget on the most likely causes of death and as a result spend little to nothing on fighting terrorism.

The wise view would seek to spend the most bang for the buck on all the various causes of death. Just about every problem meets a point of diminishing returns where more money, more resources does not help the problem at the same rate that it use to.

So we should not eliminate all spending on fighting terrorism but we should be smart about it, we should focus on the most cost effective means of fighting terrorism, and we should focus on more likely causes of death spending the lion-share of the government's budget on these endeavors.

Heart disease, cancer, diabetes, strokes, car accidents, Alzheimer's disease, influenza; these are the most likely reasons to die and should receive the lion-share of government funding, not terrorism.

Finally, it is not wise to sacrifice our freedoms to fight terrorism. The government has built a monolith of computer systems all designed to spy on everyone, foreigners, and citizens. This is a clear violation of the 4th Amendment and yet the political elite could care less. The FBI has national security letters which they can give to any business to obtain any records they want all without going before a judge and getting a warrant. Why don't these business records enjoy the same level of judicial scrutiny that paper documents in your house have. Just because we choose to do business with someone or some corporation doesn't mean those details should be freely available to the government without getting a warrant.

Hopefully congress and the political elite and the population as a whole will move away from an emotional view point to a rational or even better, wise view, on fighting terrorism in our country and throughout the world.

Chapter 33 – Growing Stupidity

My interest in forbidden technologies had not waned but I ran into a problem. Cannabis was getting harder and harder for me to get. This was before the dark markets existed like Silk Road. I decided the best way to ensure a constant supply was to grow the cannabis myself.

I ordered seeds over the internet from a store in the United Kingdom. It was supposedly easier to smuggle them through the mail from the UK than from the Netherlands. I used a prepaid credit card that I paid cash for. A got several different varieties of different potency and effect, spending about $500 on the seeds.

I decided converting one of the closets in my apartment into a grow closet was the best idea. I had read that the government uses FLIR cameras on helicopters to look for hot spots radiating from a home, tell tale heat signatures, that indicate someone growing indoors. I bought insulated foil wrapped bubble wrap for about $200 and a staple gun to staple it to the walls and ceiling. I double insulated the ceiling and outer wall, insulating the rest of the closet with one layer of insulation.

I bought three metal shelving units from Home Depot for about $75 a pop to create a two layer grow system with the growth stage in the top half and flowering stage in the bottom half. To take advantage of the space in the closet I used the parts of two of the shelving units to make one self that reached the top of the ceiling. I had to cut some of the shelf braces and drill holes in them to connect up the shelving units with bolts. It gave me a squarish grow area. I drilled holes in the cross members at the middle and top and attached chains to hang the grow light hoods from.

Because the flowering stage growth must only have light for about 12 hours a day or less I had to create shrouds to surround the growth stage and flowering stage grow areas, completely separating them.

I stupidly went to a hydroponic store to buy the grow lights, one metal halide for the growth phase and one HPS for the flowering phase. I also bought the power supplies to power the lights. This cost me around $1000. I paid cash but I went in my truck and the DEA has monitored hydroponic stores for years taking down the license plates and following the customers to their destinations, often where the grow-op is taking place. This was very poor OPSEC on my part and if I had to do it all over again I would have shopped at my local wholesale lighting store, one unlikely to be monitored by the DEA.

This choice had made me paranoid about my grow-op and it was always in the back of my mind. Never again would I visit a hydroponics store, at least not while cannabis was illegal in my state.

I used 2lb yogurt tubs to make a vent system along with dryer exhaust foil. I cut the center out of the lids and attached them to the side of the shroud. I attached the dryer foil to the grow lamp hood exhaust with a clamp and cut out the bottom of the yogurt tub and inserted it into the dryer exhaust foil. Then I simple plugged the yogurt tub into its lid.

The closet had a panel of slats that air could flow through. I used several 120mm Panaflo computer fans and constructed a cardboard frame to hold the fans against the slats and plugged in the yogurt tub in dryer foil exhaust from the shroud to the cardboard frame.

I decided I wanted to use a hydroponics setup so I used the remaining shelving unit to hold two multi-gallon bins containing a mixture of water and hydroponic fertilizer. I put shutoff valves into the bottoms of the bins'. From there I had hoses running from the shut off valves to my grow medium.

I spent about $150 on several three foot long, 5 inch by 5 inch square, PVC tubes. I cut three holes in the top facing side of each PVC tube for the cups that would hold the plants and supporting rockwool growth material. I glued the end caps onto the PVC tubes. I drilled a hole in one end cap of each tube and ran the tube from the fertilizer bins into it. Inside each PVC tube was a valve that would open when the water level was low filling up the PVC tubes automatically without me needing to monitor the water level.

Below the shelves that held the water-fertilizer bins I created a small seedling grow area with low level florescent lights I picked up at Home Depot.

I used a few seeds from a few different strains, Strawberry Cough, G13 x Hash Plant, Romulan, a land race low THC strain, and planted them in the rockwool, sticking them under the seedling light.

Chapter 34 – No Patience

It would take 8-10 weeks for the cannabis to be fully grown and I still had no weed. If I wasn't such a pot head I would have had patience and waited till the cannabis plants finished their flowering phase, but I did not. I decided to try out one of the synthetic THC compounds that were becoming popular, JWH-018. It was still legal at the time and promised a powerful high. I found a site offering the JWH-018 powder for sale, 99% pure. The site had good reviews from others so I decided to try it out. It was not like those herbal smoking packs that were spritzed with JWH-018 that are popular at head shops, it was the active ingredient in those herbal packs, pure JWH-018.

This was probably the second worst decision I made right behind growing cannabis in my closet. Figuring out how much to put in my bowl with the 99% pure JWH-018 powder was very difficult, a tiny amount of the powder was enough for a dose. Just enough to cover a tiny flat screw driver tip used for repairing eyeglasses. Only a little more or smoking too soon and not taking enough of a break would give me a terrifying experience where I would get extremely paranoid, thinking I was going to have a heart attack, curling up into a ball on the floor for half an hour.

The JWH-018 had no analogue of CBD in it, the cannabinoid that mitigates the effect of THC in cannabis, decreasing paranoia and anxiety. There was a study done by a reporter in the United Kingdom where she took THC intravenously and became extremely paranoid and psychotic but when she took the mixture of THC and CBD intravenously she was euphoric, she couldn't stop laughing, she was happy.

Getting paranoid once in a while from smoking cannabis is not too big of a deal but when you are getting high all the time and you are paranoid most of that time it starts to change your personality, your mindset changes, and your dominant mode of thinking is filled with paranoia.

It was stupid of me to have used it and it began a downfall in my psyche making me a more paranoid fearful psychotic person.

Chapter 35 – First Signs of Life

The cannabis seeds were just starting to germinate, two green leafs appeared out of the rockwool. Soon very soon I would have seedlings, bushy plants, flowers, and finally buds. In the back of my mind I was afraid, afraid of getting caught. This fear came more and more to the foreground as my plants matured. From the two initial leaves opening up from the seed, two more broad leaves erupted from the middle of the initial leaves. As time went on more recognizable cannabis leaves erupted from the middle of the plant, first three leaves, then five, and seven.

After the initial sprouting of leaves I moved the seedlings from the fluorescent lights growth area to the plant growth stage grow chamber under the powerful 300 watt metal halide light.

The smell was starting to get overpowering. You could smell the cannabis plants throughout the upstairs portion of my townhouse apartment. I had a sneaking fear that the smell was seeping through the walls invading my neighbors apartment. The grow closet did share a wall with their bedroom closet. In hindsight I should have used a different bedroom closet that was farther away from the shared wall of the apartment.

I ruminated on my neighbors calling the cops to turn me in. It didn't help that one night I heard a helicopter fly really low over my apartment and seemingly hovered over it for about thirty seconds. Was I just being paranoid? Perhaps. Or perhaps they were looking for a telltale heat signature of a cannabis indoor grow-op. Alerted by the DEA when I went to the hydroponics store or alerted by my neighbors who could smell the cannabis and called the cops.

I was confident my insulation scrambled the heat signature and all their FLIR equipment detected was a warm upstairs but at this point it really didn't matter. The smell was all encompassing, I was sure my neighbors had to smell the cannabis growing in my apartment. But I pressed on until one fateful day.

My heat was out, turning the thermostat did nothing, there was no heat to be had. I feared that somehow this was a plot to catch me growing cannabis. I had to call the building supervisors to fix the heat and once in my apartment they would likely smell the growing cannabis and turn me into the cops.

I decided to get rid of all evidence of the cannabis plants keeping the remaining seeds for perhaps sometime in the future when I could use them anew.

I cut up all the plants, removing all the barely there buds, the leaves and put that in a bag to smoke as I was desperate. The stems and other non-smokeable parts of the plants were chopped up into little bits and flushed down the toilet. Anything I couldn't flush was put in plastic bags. Wearing gloves I deposited these bags all over the city in various gas station trash cans. I wanted to leave no evidence in the apartment dumpsters as they could be monitored. The police vice squads were not above garbage picking to find evidence of cannabis in the trash, no stem too small was their modus-operandi.

I called the building supervisor and they opened the valve to my apartment turning the heat back on. The thermostat still wasn't working but I at least had heat even if it was on full blast all the time.

It was time to refocus on my main project, to forget about this stupid diversion, to build the flying car.

Chapter 36 – Still Smoking

Without a source of cannabis I continued to smoke the JWH-018 powder that I got online, I just couldn't help myself. I wanted to feel that high, that euphoria, that certainty, that comes with smoking cannabis even if it was from a research chemical whose long term effects were completely unknown. All too frequently I smoked too much of the JWH-018 getting intensely paranoid. But I still didn't stop, I was still chasing that high that I got with cannabis I smoked back in college with my roommate Jeff having great times getting stoned and playing video games or watching TV. I could be smart yet stupid at the same time.

I did press on with constructing the flying car. I worked on building the other two overunity free energy generators first as this was the easiest part of the project. An indecisive part of me wanted to test out using the higher voltage lower turns option that I had earlier dismissed. Just curiosity I guess, to see if it was the better method.

But I stuck to the plan and had bought six spools of 80 wire ribbon cable, four more 10 inch PVC end caps, two PVC tubes, four more 250 amp alternators, and two 3000 watt inverters. I bolted the alternators to the PVC end caps first and glued two of the alternator nuts on with locktite glue. I then attached the end caps to the PVC tube fitting the hex sockets together for turning the alternators with the alternator turned electric motors.

It was quicker and easier assembling the overunity generators this time around thanks to the experience I gained from the first prototype build like leaving enough of the cable sticking out at the beginning of each coil for easy wiring access. I debated buying two more UPSs as they were not cheap, not sure if I would really need them. All my computers would run through the one UPS to make sure they did not get fried but did I really need to buffer my output to the Marx generators? Perhaps a couple surge suppressor would be sufficient. I decided to shelve this decision until later.

Chapter 37 – Meeting the Defense Minister

Lu Su had arrived from his flight in North Korea. He quickly met defense minister Hyon Yong-chol. Yong-chol set up a committee of military scientists to analyze the forbidden technology intelligence Lu Su had brought with him. He wanted it understood and developed as soon as possible.

Yong-chol felt that this technology could be the key to bringing North Korea to a much grander standing on the world stage. The potential to have ICBMs, the same as the U.S., Russia, and China would raise the prestige of the country from serfdom to global nuclear military power.

Yong-chol was most interested in the forbidden propulsion technology, the Biefeld-Brown capacitors. As it was North Korea had energy technology to power an ICBM and ICBMs did not need anti-inertia technology to be a devastating weapon.

Replacing the chemical rocket component of their missiles, the area they struggled most with, with Brown capacitors could allow them to reach all corners of the earth with their nuclear weapons.

Hyon Yong-chol was a stout nationalist and if he got his way North Korea under his leadership as defense minister would be a major power in the world, pushed around by sanctions no more.

Chapter 38 – Unemployment Exhausted

My unemployment had finally run out. I could no longer afford to live in my rental townhouse in Manchester. As it was I was slowly bleeding savings while living in Manchester but now I would be totally living off of my savings and that was something I did not want to do.

It was time to move back in with my dad in Durham. I was already renting the townhouse month to month so I didn't have to break any lease or anything. I decided to rent a Uhaul, it took me a while as I had a lot of stuff but I eventually loaded it all up onto the Uhaul on the last day of the month.

I drove the Uhaul to Durham and unloaded all my stuff onto the front lawn. I took the Uhaul back to the rental center. I then proceeded to slowly bring all my stuff into the house stashing my stuff anywhere I could find space.

I tried to fit as much stuff as possible in the attic and basement where it would be out of the way and cluttering up the house as little as possible. I could not fit my king size bed into my room with my computer desk in there too.

I moved my mattress into the never used dining room. I would either sleep in the day bed downstairs or my old twin mattress in my room I have had since I was a kid.

I was determined to continue my work on the flying car even if I had to use my savings to pay for it. I did need to find a new job though and soon. Of course the downside being I would have less time to work on the flying car if I was working a 9-5 job doing whatever.

Chapter 39 – Moving Forward with the Marx Generators

I had ten Marx generators to build. It involved a ton of ceramic 30kV 100 pF capacitors, low inductance inductors and tungsten rods. Rounding over the edges of the rods was the biggest pain in the ass. The material is very hard and I used up tons of grinding wheels for my dremmel. But soldering all these tiny components together was no picnic either.

I had more than a few short circuits due to poor insulation and tight spaces, I was lucky I hadn't electrocuted myself. This really isn't for amateurs but I threw my hat over the wall and that was that. Furthermore, being high and doing delicate work do not mix.

I gave up on the ecommerce site and dedicated myself to working on the flying cars components when I got up and stopped wasting my time with an electronics store with no sales and no profits. This would allow me to wind down at night with some JWH-018 and not be pressed into soldering at all hours of the night while high.

I still visited friends on a regular basis, hung out with Steve several times a week, still got drunk several nights a week with him and my friends in Middlefield. With my lack of cannabis I was perhaps even overcompensating with my drinking but so far no real consequences so I didn't stop.

It wasn't until I woke up on the bathroom floor with puke stains on my jacket wondering how I got there that I started to question my level of drinking. My friend Steve says I tried to open the car door while he was driving so I could puke out the side of the car. I didn't remember it at all. I didn't like the feeling of not being able to remember. Sure sometimes details were fuzzy but this was a complete blackout. When you get to that point you have to ask yourself if its worth it. I wasn't ready to quit drinking but I left my flask of bourbon whiskey at home from now on and stuck to beer.

After a couple weeks I had completed the Marx generators. Unfortunately they had remained untested. I wanted a way to test them that didn't involve pulsing voltage into one of the Brown capacitors. I had to keep this project on the down low and doing more demos in fields would get riskier and riskier each time.

Chapter 40 – Testing the Marx Generators

I decided the best way to test the Marx generator was to set up a grounding rod. I would move my working Marx generator near the rod. While active the Marx generator will arc to the grounding rod. Now by moving the Marx generator farther and farther away from the rod between tests I got my total distance away from the grounding rod that my working prototype generator could do which I knew was powerful enough to propel the Biefeld-Brown flat parallel plate capacitor.

I then placed my other Marx generators that same distance to test if they were putting out the level of voltage I needed. The farther it arcs, the higher the voltage. To test the firing rate of the Marx generators I needed a high speed camera, one that could take hundreds of frames a second so I could check out how often the Marx generators were sending out voltage pulses.

I found a low cost high speed camera online, the FPS1000. It can capture 550 frames per second at 720P resolution for $480. Expensive for a tool I will not use again, at least that I know of, but I don't have a choice. I have to make sure I can dial in the voltage pulse rates into the capacitors with the trigatrons.

All of the Marx generators were assembled the same, luckily they all performed like the prototype.

It was now time to move on to making the Brown flat parallel plate capacitors.

Chapter 41 – Conspiracy Theory Part Deux

Max Spiers was a hardcore conspiracy theorist. He believed in many far out ideas, fringe ideas and apparently he was killed for one of them.

Max Spiers, father of two, was found dead in an apartment he was staying at shortly before he was to give a presentation at a paranormal conference in Poland. His roommate found him earlier puking up a black liquid. While it is possible that he had died from some kind of stomach problem and the black liquid was coagulated blood he sounded an alarm bell days before he died.

Max Spiers had sent a text to his mother a few days before his death stating 'that if anything happened to him to investigate it'. Max Spiers had received numerous death threats during his investigating and reporting which lead me to believe that he was onto something or somethings.

Max Spiers delved into many conspiracy subjects including reptilians being on earth. The theory goes that all humans have human and reptile DNA in them. Those with over 50% reptilian DNA are shape shifters. That many of the prominent people including the Royal family in Britain and the Bush family in America are reptilians.

Their supposed agenda is to takeover the planet covertly, infiltrating society by shape shifting into human looking individuals and infiltrating places of power.

Personally I don't give much credence to this conspiracy theory and doubt he would have been killed for espousing it but it does have its supporters. Personally if I was an alien trying to live my life on earth I wouldn't want to make it known myself, I wouldn't want to be hunted down for being different. Numerous stories of Big Foot or alien visitation include tales of shooting at these beings. Our society would have to fundamentally change for species to cohabitate with us out in the open and not fear death from some scared human with a gun.

Another of his theories is a human experimentation lab creating human/alien hybrids in an underground base called Dulce Base by human and extraterrestrial teams. Spiers is not the first person to make this claim, a man by the name of Phil Schnieder also talked about Dulce Base and a human alien battle that occurred in it. He claimed to have been an engineer who helped build the base and he too died under mysterious circumstances. Schneider's body was found with ligature marks on the neck which appeared to have been made by a rubber hose found at the scene.

I give this conspiracy theory more credit as to being the cause for Spiers' murder, especially because of Phil Schneider who made the same claims and also died under mysterious circumstances.

Spiers believed in a Fourth Reich, a secret continuation of the Nazi agenda. He believed they were conducting mind control experiments and that he was one of their victims. I have no idea to the validity of this theory. Any X-Files fan is probably familiar with Operation Paperclip that brought Nazi scientists to America to help us win the Cold War with the USSR but that is a far cry from a secret Nazi organization attempting to control the world.

Potentially the most scary conspiracy theory Spiers proposed was his belief in a society of people that ruled the world using Black Satanic magic. The speech he was supposed to give at the conference in Poland was about this subject. Who knows if he was naming names, he did say there were celebrities and politicians that were members of this group.

Seeing how his death was right before he was to give this presentation it does make one wonder if this was the conspiracy theory that got him murdered. And if so it makes one think no one is safe from their black magic, that they can kill with it and have done so. Or perhaps he was just poisoned, a conventional explanation that is more plausible to me. Either way though it shows if someone wants you dead they can find a way and someone or someones wanted Spiers dead for espousing some conspiracy theories that were on the mark.

Spiers reminds me of Jerry in the movie Conspiracy Theory with Mel Gibson. He too espoused many conspiracy theories most of which were bunk but all it took was for one to be right to get Jerry hunted and if the autopsy on Max Spiers turns up with murder by poison at least one of his theories was true.

Chapter 42 – The North Korea Situation

Homeworld Security's satellites had detected Biefeld-Brown flat parallel plate capacitor anomalies in North Korea coming from one of their military installations. The department was in a tizzy. Nothing of Brown capacitor discussion in North Korea was detected by Project Luddite's feeds. Their experiments had seemingly come out of the blue. Anything was possible perhaps they stumbled upon some of the conspiracies on the internet, ARV lore or one of the few papers on the subject, but Bill Armstrong believed they got their information from somewhere else.

The internet is so restricted in the country that it is unlikely a high level North Korean military officer would have found the information on forum discussions, never mind read English. Armstrong had to consider the possibility of a defector. In his eyes too many people already know about the technology. He didn't have to worry about just an American defector but Great Britain, France, Russia, and China.

If he had to bet he would bet on China. China is North Korea's virtually only real ally and even that is largely a one sided relationship. That said China's official government had no interest in North Korea unleashing this propulsion technology to the world and distributing it to countries like Iran. Their had to be a defector, someone in the know, at least about the basics if not about the actual craft in service. A lone wolf operating outside their country's leadership.

Armstrong had work to do. He had to determine who in China would be in the know and all the people in China who had gone to North Korea in the recent time.

Chapter 43 – The Death of Phil Schneider

Phil Schneider was an engineer who attended UFO panels giving speeches about a DUMB, deep underground military base. He claims to have worked on one in Dulce, New Mexico. He claimed humans and aliens had a confrontation in this base resulting in many deaths. His speeches at UFO conferences can still be found on Youtube. He stated that there were tons of DUMBs throughout the country for important people to live and work if something catastrophic happened to the country or the earth.

The Dulce base is said to be a place of genetic experimentation in an attempt to create human/alien hybrids with the Greys.

Homeworld Security did not want this idea to gain traction with the UFO public or the public at large. They did not feel that society would understand such experimentation. Some reports have stated that the Greys. are sterile due to degradation of their DNA from cloning and radiation. That the attempts to create hybrids are to allow the Grey species to reproduce again.

Others state that the hybrid program was an effort to make changes in the DNA of modern humans to advance us along as they had done for millennia.

Homeworld Security tasked a hit squad to murder Schneider before he gained more traction with his tales. Phil Schneider was found dead in his apartment with ligature marks on his throat. A rubber hose was found at the scene and is believed to have been the murder weapon. Ironically like Obi Wan Kenobi in Star Wars, in death these whistle blowers become more powerful than they ever were alive. The death of a conspiracy theorist causes UFO and paranormal researchers to give their theories far more weight than they ever would if they were still alive.

Chapter 44 – Seeing Eye Soon to be All

Bill Armstrong had pressed the All Seeing Eye development team into overdrive. They had gotten a lead on the rogue Chinese military officer, a Lu Su, who was the number one suspect of conducting the espionage for North Korea.

Unfortunately we still didn't have a solid grip on the North Korean military infrastructure and communications systems. It was one of the NSA's biggest blind spots.

They were still detecting gravitational anomalies in the North Korean military facility. Homeworld Security considered bombing the facility or sending in a strike team but the fallout could be a nuclear war in the Korean peninsula. Furthermore there was no telling whether they had other experiments being developed in other sites or had offsite storage of the information.

Homeworld Security was lucky in that North Korea lacked many of the basic supplies necessary to construct quality capacitors. The country only had low quality epoxy and no access to G10 dielectric. China's members in Homeworld Security had promised to prevent any epoxy or G10 from being exported from China to North Korea. North Korea did not have much in the way of trading partners besides China.

Bill Armstrong wanted All Seeing Eye done yesterday but version 1.0 was almost finished and he couldn't wait until it was in the field ferreting out all of North Korean communications and electronics, not to mention the systems in the rest of the world. Maybe he would be able to finally track down the anomaly in Connecticut as well.

Chapter 45 – Constructing the Frame

My flying car was going to be lightweight yet strong. I was inspired by motorcycles, I decided to use chrome molly steel tubes for the frame with bolt holes for mounting the Biefeld-Brown parallel plate capacitors, body plates, and other parts. This should make for a strong enough frame to handle the propulsion of the Brown capacitors. The flying car would be mainly a triangular shape with a triangular dome in the middle for the single pilot seat.

I do not have the welding skills to pull it off, never mind a welding machine.

I would have to outsource the construction of the frame to an experienced welder, someone at a motorcycle shop would work well. They often have extensive metal fabrication capabilities in those shops, they shouldn't have a problem welding together the flying car frame.

But that means I would definitely need a CAD blueprint to give them and it would have to be fully designed. No leaving metal brackets or other frame components off the blueprint.

I do not have any CAD skills either so it was time to study. A full complete blueprint of the entire craft would be quite the challenge but without it I would just be mickey mousing the thing together and would conceivably have to hire the welder for multiple jobs instead of just one.

Since I have no CAD experience at all I am free in that I am not tied down to a single program like AutoCAD a very popular but expensive CAD program. Since I am no longer a pirate that would not do. I did a little research and found an open source free 3D CAD program called FreeCAD. It has a large support base and is very flexible. This won't be like a little detective work googling and reading, it will be more like learning a programming language, or learning to program from scratch.

Time to get studying.

Chapter 46 – Death of an American Congressman

Congressman Steven Schiff sat on the committee overseeing the GAO (General Accounting Office). In that position he decided to pursue the issue of the Roswell crash in his state of New Mexico in 1947. He wanted to find any records including fiscal expenditures by the military related to the Roswell incident.

At first Congressman Schiff contacted the Department of Defense but they were not forthcoming with any information related to Roswell. As a result Schiff used his power overseeing the GAO to request that the GAO provide him information on the Roswell incident.

He asked to see the incoming and outgoing communications of the Roswell military base during the Roswell incident. There were several communications that had simply disappeared. They had been destroyed without approval. These communications were supposed to be archived. This is highly suspicious considering the military later claimed that it was a test rig designed to detect nuclear explosions. They want us to believe that they seemingly retained those records but for some reason some of the records about this test rig were destroyed. Why would they do that? If however there really was a crash of a UFO at Roswell it makes much more sense that they would have destroyed those records.

There were no fiscal records related to Roswell at all related to the recovery of the crashed object, another stonewall

Congressman Schiff acquired skin cancer while in office pursuing the Roswell incident and died from it. He is not alone in dying from a fast acting skin cancer or other cancers.

Steven Greer a UFO researcher and medical doctor with a checkered reputation and his right hand assistant Shari Adiamack both acquired a fast acting skin cancer at the same time while they were looking into the UFO story. Greer survived but Adiamack did not.

Greer related a story where he was with Adiamack and a dog and a vehicle drove up aiming some sort of device, potentially a microwave cancer weapon, and all three including the dog came down with skin cancer soon after.

Project Luddite has numerous weapons at their disposal to cause fatal diseases in regular people and make it look like death by natural causes as a way to avoid increased scrutiny in these peoples' cases. A murder by gunshot to the head brings an investigation, death by skin cancer gets no scrutiny at all.

Chapter 47 – Making Progress on the CAD File

My initial outline of the flying car was done, the bare bones of the frame. FreeCAD was pretty intuitive, I was making progress at a decent rate. From there I would be able to mount plates to the frame to the mounting holes myself.

I still needed to design the canopy and the metal frame the canopy rests on, where the canopy locks down onto the frame.

I also needed to design the monitor mounting brackets where the interior computer screens would mount. They have monitor mounts for sale but they are made for mounting to wall studs. There would obviously be no wall studs in the flying car. I decided that I would design the bracket that would attach to the cockpit that all my interior computer monitors would mount to.

I would have a monitor for a front view, two side monitors for the left and right sides of the craft and two monitors, one above the main one and one below for a view above and below the craft. Designing the mounts would be a bit tricky.

I also needed to design the mounting boxes for the Biefeld-Brown parallel plate capacitors. I already had my prototype Brown capacitor and Marx generator unit available with which to design a box around that would mount to the base flying car frame. It would have to fit like a glove, the last thing I would want is for the Brown capacitor to be rattling around in the box.

This gave me an idea, I would place the Brown capacitors in their boxes and then fill it with epoxy to take up the entire space in the metal boxes. With the Marx generators I would place them in metal boxes filled with transformer oil so I could easily remove them and repair them if any of the components break down while still providing a barrier to prevent electricity from arcing somewhere it doesn't belong.

One last thing, I needed to mount the speaker horns somewhere on the flying car frame so I had to design a mounting bracket for that as well.

Still more work to do but making progress.

Chapter 48 – North Korean Progress

Hyon Yong-chol's committee was making progress with the Biefeld-Brown parallel plate capacitors research group. They were getting propulsive effects but the dielectrics were weak and impure. They tended to short out after a little use.

Hyon Yong-chol had contacted his associate from China looking for help with procuring high quality dielectrics. His requests however were rebuffed as attempts to ship high quality epoxies met with red tape and obstacles until he was finally told such substances would no longer be shipped to North Korea. It appeared than China was joining the rest of the U.N. Security Council rather than with North Korea as they had in the past.

Hyon Yong-chol was however able to get silicon dioxide powder which would improve the dielectric strength of the epoxy albeit making it more difficult to work with, thicker and reducing the time it takes for the epoxy to cure, to solidify. Yong-chol was also able to get some strong vacuum pumps and industrial vacuum chambers which would be useful in quickly degassing the epoxy.

Yong-chol was confident that very soon he would have a working Brown capacitor attached to a conventional missile warhead for testing. It was just a matter of time until they got the mixture of silicon dioxide right in the epoxy.

From there larger and larger warheads would be tested until finally they are ready to mount a nuclear weapon to the Brown capacitor.

Chapter 49 – Bloodbath

I took to IRC and began telling a chat room of 2600 members about the technology and my experiment. I told them I needed help, that the government was on to me. I might just have been paranoid from the encounter at Pepe's. That had been a while ago but every day that I worked on the flying car project I got more and more paranoid that the government was on to me and would drop the hammer on me soon, very soon.

One member asked for video so I uploaded the test in the field to the chatroom. Some wondered if I had somehow cheated, suspended the device by a wire. Others thought I was onto something. The participant who asked for the video upload said he would get back to me.

Around 10pm a car pulled up into the driveway. A man got out who I recognized as Emmanuel Goldstein and walked to my front door. I opened the door and he said to me that he was from 2600 and that he wanted me to go for a ride. I was skeptical, I had not given out my address, I don't know how he found me but I trusted him. On his radio show he was clearly an activist and spoke truth to power.

There was something about him that made him seem genuine. I decided to trust him, he said he was taking me to meet the other 2600 members he knew and to devise a plan. I took my USB stick with my FreeCAD drawing of the flying car I had been designing.

It was a several hour drive but we pulled up to a warehouse in NYC. He knocked on the door but there was no answer. He got suspicious and unlocked the door and proceeded into the warehouse. We found a horrific scene, about a dozen 2600 members had been shot dead, blood all over the place. The chatroom had been monitored and the meeting place compromised.

If they could kill a bunch of people for seeing a video what would they do to the man, me, who created the experimental prototype or my family.

I insisted he take me back home. He was adamant that that was a bad idea but I had to make sure my family, my dad, was OK. It was a long drive back, fear and uncertainty filled my bones. I just hoped, prayed, that my dad was OK.

We arrived back in Durham, CT where the prototype was, to find police, fire, and EMTs at the scene. As I approached the scene and asked a police officer what had happened he stated that it was a robbery gone bad. My father was dead, shot in the back of the head. They would not let me in the house but I sneaked around to the side of the house where the basement door was.

I unlocked the door and found that my prototypes were gone.

It was only a matter of time now before they found me and killed me. They probably conducted the robbery because they thought I was home with my truck in the driveway. Getting in Goldstein's car probably saved my life.

I decided to leave with the 2600 member. He was the only one with an ability to keep me safe. I needed to leave the country and go into hiding. He stated that he knew people in Europe who could hide me.

Chapter 50 – 1984 Is Here, Welcomed Into Our Lives

1984, a book and a movie, one or both ought to be viewed at least once. It details a man living in Oceania (U.S. and U.K.), a member of the single ruling party who lives in a society with no privacy.

All TVs and monitors have cameras and microphones built in allowing the government to see and listen in on your activities in your own home. The protagonist writes in a journal in a corner of his apartment where the telescreen can't see, the tiny amount of privacy he can have. This book really changed my outlook on technology and how present technology gives our government the same power that Oceania had in 1984.

Cellphones can not just have calls monitored keeping tabs on who you call and what you say during your conversations but the microphone can be remotely turned on by the government right now so they can listen in on you while you are in your home and not making any calls at all. If you find you have battery problems, it draining quick, its possible that your mic is being remotely turned on.

If the camera is out of your pocket it can see through its camera into your home as well. These are powers the government currently has, its not just part of a dystopian book, it is our current reality.

Webcams on laptops and on some monitors or 3rd party webcams offer the government the same capabilities all without reducing the battery life on your device like with what happens with a cellphone when they turn on remote listening.

Amazon Fire Stick, it now has a microphone, as does Xfinity's latest cable box remote. How do prevent the microphone from listening to everything being said in the room? You can't, not without hacking the device and putting in a physical switch that cuts off the microphone. These companies will say they do not spy on you but there is nothing to stop the government from coming in and spying on you through those devices without you even knowing about it, without anyone in government notifying you about it.

Amazon Echo and Google Home are but the first in a line of products filled with microphones which can be made to listen at all times and record your conversations in your home. Far better at spying than a webcam and mic on a laptop, or cellphone in a pocket, or remote for a cable box, these devices employ multiple microphones to provide a better user experience and allow the Echo or Home to hear you regardless of where you are in the room.

But the better the product is, the better snoop it will be when government decides they want to listen to your conversations in your home and own your device.

We are inviting these technologies into our homes without much thought as to how they could be used against us. Essentially we are inviting these spies into our homes, the government need not force it down our throats like in 1984, we buy this technology willingly.

Now I know some of you will say if you have nothing to hide you have nothing to fear. Don't be so sure. I didn't have something to hide, I was working on forbidden technology, something completely legal even though those who do are persecuted. The more who put these potential snooping devices in their homes, the more who don't will stand out, the more likely they will be put on a list and the more likely they will be unable to do research on forbidden technology or whatever else they are looking to uncover. As a result I have no snooping devices that can be remotely turned on to spy on me but that makes me an outlier.

If product manufacturers are serious about our privacy then they need to implement physical switches in products with cameras, microphones, and GPSs to turn them off when we don't want to risk being monitored. You used to be able to at least take the battery out of your cellphone turning off its snooping capabilities but even that is gone from the most popular phones like Apple iPhones and Samsung Galaxy Ss.

It is up to us to vote with our dollars. If you want to risk being spied on, I hope you aren't cheating on your spouse or significant other. I hope you are not using drugs or selling them, not even cannabis. I hope you aren't doing research in areas that the government doesn't want you to like I am cause if the government official wants to they can ruin your life or even take it.

Your actions on the internet are recorded forever. Forget about uploading that video to Youtube of your forbidden technology prototype, they can and will drop the hammer on you. Even TOR is likely compromised and while I advocate its use as it is the best anonymous internet tool we have, I have no idea if it is safe.

Chapter 51 – Wetworks of One

Armstrong of Project Luddite was just getting the situation report on his tactical mission to eliminate those who knew of the forbidden technology video. Their NSA feed had caught a video upload in an IRC chat room showing a capacitor lifting off the ground at high speed.

One of the chat participants, Robert Francis, was on their monitored list for some time after calling for experiments to be done on supposed forbidden technology. He was the one who uploaded the video. He must be the one who have conducted the experiment in the field in Connecticut. He had to be eliminated.

Two teams were dispatched, one to Durham, to eliminate Robert Francis and his father who lived with him, the other to a warehouse in New York where members of the hacker community 2600 who witnessed the video were congregating.

Unfortunately the operation in Durham missed its target. The technology prototypes, computers, and notebooks were recovered but Robert Francis was not home, his truck though still in the driveway.

The operation on the warehouse eliminated most of the members who saw the video but not their ring leader named after the protagonist in 1984, Emmanuel Goldstein, a man, a hacktivist, they had been monitoring for a long time.

As Armstrong chewed out his subordinate for not making sure Francis was home, he got an idea. He would put both men on the terrorist watch list. They would be picked up at any bus station, train station, subway, airport, or at the border. Armstrong had to tighten the noose and capture the men as quickly as possible. He could not afford any more screw ups.

Project All Seeing Eye would have contained this outbreak. It would have analyzed the uploading video and scrambled it before the chat members could see it. It would have seen all vehicles that left the Durham site and tracked them to their destinations with the red light cameras filling the nations roadway intersections.

Armstrong was more determined than ever to bring Project All Seeing Eye online, to contain the threats of forbidden technology being spread and give its handler the targets to eliminate. This debacle was getting away from Armstrong and he had to get it under control or else his future would be much more uncertain than just a few days ago.

Chapter 52 – Terror Alert Level Raised

The terrorist alert level had been raised and Robert and Emmanuel's faces were plastered on every 24 hour news and local news station throughout the tri-state area. Pictures taken from their drivers licenses showed prominently on TV screens everywhere as cable news readers read their teleprompters, this terrorist farce just beginning.

From Anderson Cooper on CNN to Rachel Madow on MSNBC to Bill O'Reilly on Fox News they all covered a blood bath in an NYC warehouse being blamed on the terrorists Robert Francis and Emmanuel Goldstein. The motive was a statement to put fear in the hearts of America's tech elite. An audio recording found at the scene had Goldstein pledging support for the elimination of all artificial intelligences and those working on them. The recording spouted gloom and doom, that if AI was allowed to develop it would one day takeover the world and eliminate the human race and that no one who worked on AI was safe, not Google, not IBM, not Microsoft, not Amazon, no one. That this necessary purge had just begun.

Some news pundits were again calling for stricter gun controls, that lone wolf terrorists were slipping through the cracks and terrorizing

America. Others were calling for increased gun ownership to combat these terrorists when they decide to attack.

It was the usual three ring circus.

It didn't matter that Goldstein had hosted a radio show, was a peaceful activist, few remembered that, most never hearing his radio show or knowing the man at all. The government sure did though and they used his radio show podcasts to make the fake speech that was found by local police on the scene at the warehouse.

There was an all points bulletin out for Goldstein and Francis throughout NYC. Police had the make and model of his car and were on the lookout with their crude but effective license plate scanners. With this technology in their squad cars they could keep track of every individual driving past them. It was only a matter of time before they found Goldstein's vehicle and brought the duo to 'justice'.

Chapter 53 – Finding an Exit

Goldstein and I were driving back to New York City. The plan was to escape the country aboard a cargo freighter. Goldstein knew a Captain, Hans Drexler, through an acquaintance and he could be counted upon to smuggle us out of the country.

Goldstein got a text message on his burner phone from a close friend not at the warehouse informing him of our terrorist status. As we mulled our options I told him to pullover into a commuter ride sharing parking lot. Goldstein kept a few basic tools in his trunk and with them we swapped license plates with one of the vehicles in the parking lot.

This should buy us some time, a police officer would have to look into the records of the plate to determine that the tags don't match the car. Thankfully we don't yet have license plate scanners that also image the make, model, and color of the vehicle to see if they match with the records of the license plate.

We resumed our journey to NYC and the Red Hook Container Terminal driving the speed limit, trying to blend in and be anonymous.

Goldstein parked the car in a garage and we hoofed it on foot. As we walked on foot to the terminal a police officer was directing traffic at the intersection. Goldstein could feels the officer's eyes upon him. He looked just like his license photo, I on the other hand was clean shaven except a goatee, finally cleaning up from a giant beard and a scraggly bald head. Goldstein whispered to me to keep on walking no matter what, the container terminal's cranes already in sight.

As a group of New Yorkers crossed the intersection the officer confronted Goldstein. He was made. I kept on walking but Goldstein ran in another direction. Certain that he would die no matter what he did, he led the officer, who had pulled his gun, away from the terminal, back to Brooklyn.

A few shots rang out but I kept my head down and kept walking not seeing if Goldstein was hit. I had dragged him into my mess and now he might be dead because of me, like my father.

Getting on the boat was not straight forward. The container terminal was swarming with giant machines loading and unloading cargo containers. Finally I ran into a worker and asked for directions to the boat with Captain Hans Drexler. I stated I was a friend and he offered to give me a tour of his state of the art cargo freighter. The worker brought me to Drexler. I stated I was a friend of Mr Goldstein. When Drexler asked me what had happened to Emmanuel I just told him that he didn't make it that I wasn't sure if he was still alive. When the coast was clear Hans Drexler unlocked one of the cargo containers and took me inside. There was a few weeks worth of water, MREs, and a flash light. There was a bucket to relieve myself in the corner. It was not the Astoria in New York City but it would do in getting me to Germany where I could slip into the country anonymously.

I couldn't believe I was leaving America. It was my home. It is one of the best countries in the world despite all the wars and corruption. I wanted to believe that the American Dream was real but clearly it wasn't. Not if you pushed against those in power, trying to reveal something they had kept hidden for seventy years. Just think about it, for seventy years they have suppressed any public knowledge of their research into propellantless propulsion, anti-gravity and anti-inertia, and free energy. They act outside the law in dealing with any experimenters and even just witnesses, killing them all to keep it secret.

It was time to move on, I had to leave, leaving my remaining family behind, unable to contact them again without risking exposure.

I threw my hat over the wall and now was not the time to give up, not after what I had lost, my dad, what Goldstein possibly lost, his life. I grabbed my USB stick with the plans to my flying car design and my experimental data and put it back in my pocket. Drexler closed the container door, the loud metal on metal clanking shut.

Chapter 54 – What Day is It?

Time dragged on in that cargo container. It was like being in solitary in prison I imagined. No one to talk to, nothing to do to keep the mind occupied. I didn't know what time or even day it was. I tried to ration my water and MREs not wanting to die of dehydration halfway across the Atlantic Ocean.

I was getting stir crazy. I sat in all darkness on the cold metal floor. Then it hit me, something I hadn't done in a long time, meditate.

Instead of fantasizing and thinking about anything and everything, mostly ruminating on the flying car, I let it all go and tried to quiet my mind. I focused on my back against the wall of the container as I breathed in and out, in and out. People go to retreats to sit in peace and quiet and meditate for hours, days on end. I was getting the freebie version and it didn't suck.

Meditation is supposed to have positive effects on the doer such as increased focus and attention span, a quieting of the mind over time, increased IQ, and overall well being.

Finally we pulled into port in Germany and the roar of the diesel engines quieted. I waited patiently for the Captain to unlock and open the cargo container hoping that he hadn't forgotten about me.

After a few hours of more meditation I heard the container unlock and the doors opened. Captain Drexler walked in and gave me a crewman's uniform telling me to put it on. Now was not the time to be shy, I changed my clothes quickly and he led me out of the container and off the ship.

There was a man with a car waiting for me as I reached the port's gates, he could have been a spitting image of Jason Statham.

"Mr Goldstein and his associates instructed me to take you to Switzerland outside Geneva."

I followed the driver to his car and got in the back seat.

"You will set up shop in an old plastics factory where you can resume your work. Here is a notepad, make a grocery list and I will deliver them on a weekly basis."

"I will stop by weekly and personally handle your projects material requirements as well."

I proceeded to tell the driver that I needed a laptop, preferably a desktop with a couple monitors. That I had some CAD drawings and would like to pay a local metal shop to construct the chrome molly steel tube frame.

"Everything will be taken care of." he assured me.

Chapter 55 – The New Digs

The journey to Switzerland was uneventful taking about eight hours. Police here were not looking for me thankfully. If I played my part right, they would never know I was here. I exited the vehicle and went inside the factory. Inside was a small bed in what was the break room along with a microwave and refrigerator. There was however no oven.

Looks like I was gonna have to add a George Foreman grill to the list to cook up burgers for myself.

On the factory floor there was a workstation set up with a dual monitor desktop system running Qubes Linux, one of the most secure Linux operating systems. I couldn't use my old Hulu and Netflix accounts, maybe they could give me a Hulu and Netflix login.

I downloaded and fired up FreeCAD plugging my USB memory stick into the back of the computer, backing up my USB stick to the computer and then deleting all the files. My first step to building a flying car was the frame, something I had no welding experience for. I exported the frame of the model flying car into an AutoCAD compatible file and put the copy on the USB stick.

The driver was still there as I told him to hang around for a little bit. I handed him the USB stick and told him to go to a motorcycle shop, that they would be able to weld the frame together for me.

I also handed him a grocery list of pasta salad, broccoli, hamburger, cheese, bacon, potato rolls, a tomato, and lettuce.

"What do people who don't speak Swiss do around here for fun?"

"Drink alone."

"The Chrome browser on the computer already has a Netflix and Hulu login installed."

"You're a step ahead of me."

"You can not leave the factory until the plan is in its final stage. There is no telling who might see you or what a satellite might pick up. Remain here at all times."

I was beginning to feel claustrophobic, already I was to remain in a confined space. However it was not that different from what I was living with at home in America. But no IM chats with friends during the day, no going to a bar for drinks with friends, no cannabis. I was unsure how I would handle the isolation. Binge-watching Netflix was my only recreational outlet and other than visits by driver I had no social outlet at all.

I had to toughen up. I threw my hat over the wall and I am not gonna let a little isolation stop me. This flying car will be built and I will land at the 50 yard line during the Super Bowl. It had to happen, it was going to happen, it will happen.

Chapter 56 – No Sign of Terrorist Robert Francis

Emmanuel Goldstein had been shot and killed by the police officer who spotted him, no arrest, no trial, no founding of guilt, executed by an increasingly militarized police force doing the bidding unknowingly of Project Luddite. But there was no trace of Robert Francis the principle target. Neither Bill Armstrong, nor his subordinates knew what had happened to him, he simply disappeared without a trace.

The police did find Goldstein's car in a parking lot, if Francis was with him then he was likely in the city which caused the mayor of the city to petition the President to raise the terror alert level again. If Francis wasn't with Goldstein when he came back to New York City, he could be anywhere. Most likely in the areas around Durham, Middletown, Rocky Hill, Wallingford, Meriden given that he had no form of transportation. If he did somehow find transportation, stealing a car for example, he could be anywhere.

It was doubtful that Francis would've gone into the woods or a park, he had no nature survival skills, he would never be able to forage for water, food, and shelter out in the wilderness. He had to be holed up somewhere or on the run.

All Seeing Eye was almost ready, it was a matter of days. If Robert Francis appeared in front of any cameras Project Luddite would know. As it was they were running a search on grocery store databases they had access to, to search for individuals buying foods Francis had been buying at his local Stop & Shop before they had dropped the hammer. It was a long shot but they were hoping to find the pattern somewhere, anywhere, any lead they could possibly uncover.

As far as Armstrong knew from the data accumulated on Francis he did not have a supply of cash nor valuables he could pawn for cash. They were actively monitoring for use of his credit and debit cards but so far no hits.

Armstrong had to accept the possibility that he was being helped, perhaps by a friend or associate letting him stay at their place or supplying him with food. Armstrong tasked the FBI with interviewing his friends and associates to see if they have seen Francis, monitoring them to make sure he wasn't in their homes.

Chapter 57 – Flying Car Frame

I was cooking up a bacon cheeseburger on the Foreman Grill when driver arrived. He was driving a small moving truck. He backed up to the dock and rolled open the door.

Inside was the flying car frame I had designed. It looked ready to go. Other than the flying car frame I was starting entirely from scratch. I had to start over in building the Biefeld-Brown flat parallel plate capacitors, Marx generators, and overunity free energy alternator generators. I gave the driver a list of materials I needed:

Marx generator:

30kV ceramic capacitors, inductors, blind drilled tungsten balls, clear flexible plastic tubing, aquarium sealant, 30kV DC flyback transformers, trigatrons, diodes, mosfets, electrical plugs, FPS1000 video camera, and Arduinos;

Biefeld-Brown flat parallel plate capacitors:

G10 dielectric, 1/2" copper plates, high dielectric strength clear epoxy, a vacuum chamber, and three chambered metal boxes to create a form for the Brown capacitors and mount them along with the Marx generators to the flying car;

Anti-gravity/Anti-inertia System

150kV wire cable spools, 30kV AC flyback transformers, 30kV ceramic capacitors, diodes, mosfets, electrical plugs;

Overunity free energy generators:

10" pipe end caps, 10" foot long pipes, 250 amp alternators, 150kV wire cable spools, 30kV AC flyback transformers, 30kV ceramic capacitors, diodes, mosfets, electrical plugs, 24 volt power supplies, 12 volt DC to 120 volt AC 3000 watt inverters;

Navigation:

ups battery backup, a few raspberry pi 3s, NoIR filter raspberry pi Csi video cameras, a few Arduinos, a GPS module, a USB flight stick and throttle, a keyboard and trackball for the navigation and flight control, and cockpit view screens for the flying car;

Interior:

racing seat, canopy gasket, canopy pressure locks

Exterior Speakers:

three horn loudspeakers for broadcasting my message at the Super Bowl.

The driver stated that he would need to make multiple purchases with multiple identities shipped to multiple addresses to avoid scrutiny from the NSA who might correlate the items with building forbidden technology. That it would take a few weeks but he would deliver the items as he got them on the once a week schedule.

So as I sat and twiddled my thumbs with no work to do I fired up Hulu and watched some Stargate SG-1, one of my favorite sci-fi shows. It resembled the world we live in much more accurately than Star Trek, Star Wars, or Babylon 5 for better or worse.

The Raspberry Pis and Arduinos were the first to arrive at week two. I got to work writing code for the Arduinos to put them in control of the trigatron pulse rates. I would have to interface the USB flight sticks to the Arduinos. No experience there so I had a lot of research to do on connecting the flight sticks to the Arduinos so that when I move the flight stick left the left down capacitor activates and the right up capacitor activates and vice versa for tilting right. Throttle would be connected to pulse rate of all capacitors.

Instead of connecting the USB connector to the raspberry pi, it might be better to take the raw signals from the flight stick and throttle and direct them into the Arduino analog pins.

I also wanted to be able to enter a course using the keyboard and GPS so somehow I had to interface the raspberry pi with the GPS and control the Arduinos with a higher level program. Definitely not straightforward and definitely not in my area of expertise. Ground scanning also had to be a part of things or I might fly to low and hit a tree or building.

Unfortunately I have not received the laser sensors to monitor flight level and ground distance so interfacing them with the Arduinos and raspberry pis was not possible; regardless of my ability to code those requirements.

Chapter 58 – All Seeing Eye Online

Bill Armstrong was almost gleeful, All Seeing Eye was online, soon enough he would find Robert Francis and take him out. All Seeing Eye was literally everywhere.

All public cameras worldwide were online and being fed into All Seeing Eye. All Seeing Eye was running facial recognition against every person on every camera in the world. Malicious firmware was being distributed by zero day vulnerabilities in commonly used browsers to internet users across the internet infecting motherboards, hard drives, graphics cards, network cards, USB memory sticks; as well as insecure IoT (Internet of Things) devices like thermostats with WiFi and private network security cameras.

Once the firmware was in place it could bypass operating system protections and download larger malicious packages that bury themselves in the host operating system to fully spy on all activity on a computer reporting back to Project Luddite anything they were looking for.

The only systems in the world they wouldn't be able to access were air-gapped systems but even those could be compromised if a malicious USB stick was used with the air-grapped system and all USB sticks were to be infected so it was mostly just a matter of time.

Chapter 59 – Metal Boxes

I needed to attach the Biefeld-Brown flat parallel plate capacitors and Marx generators to the flying car frame. I couldn't run bolts through the epoxy in the Brown capacitors it would weaken it and electricity would likely arc to the bolts.

I needed some durable metal boxes with air tight lids. The metal boxes were to be partitioned into three compartments that I could place the Brown capacitors in the center compartments and the positive and negative Marx generators in the inside and outside compartments. I needed to be able to bolt the metal boxes to the frame. I needed durable so I went with stainless steel.

I fired up FreeCAD and exported a design of a metal box with flanges on it that I had created earlier that would bolt to the frame. I needed six of them, one for each Brown capacitor and Marx generator combo.

I gave my list of needed items as well as the FreeCAD drawing on a USB stick to Driver during his weekly visit.

Driver had been having some trouble finding trigatrons. They aren't really used anymore except for Marx generators and not too many people build Marx generators among the civilian public. I advised him to look to China, they likely can make them for a reasonable price like the 30kV 200 watt flyback transformers I use in powering the Marx generators.

Speaking of which I added identical flyback transformers to the list, a total of twenty four of them. Four flybacks per Marx generator for six Marx generators. This should allow me to put some wattage into the Brown capacitors.

I still hadn't decided on what kind of wire to use to make the multifilar coil that would surround the cockpit and when activated would reduce inertia in the cockpit; allowing me to accelerate and stop at great speeds. Sure, I used ribbon cable around the overunity free energy alternators but I never did try using thicker high voltage wire, something in the 30kV or 150kV range that could be powered by additional flyback transformers.

Perhaps the answer was in using a normal electromagnetic coil calculator. One that would take in the number of turns, the length of the wire, the voltage, and determine the strength of the coil. While I am building a multifilar coil where voltage not current is important, the opposite of a normal electromagnetic coil, a normal electromagnetic coil calculator might not be useful. Unfortunately there were no multifilar or bifilar coil calculators. Maybe I could try using Tesla's bifilar coil formula.

Doing a quick comparison I checked how many 300V ribbon cable wires would fit where one 30kVwould. There would be 16 ribbon cable wires versus one high voltage wire. Couldn't tell you if this is right but 16 * 300V is 4800V, well short of 30kV.

On eBay companies were selling 30kV and 150kV wire. The 150kV wire was 8mm in diameter, a little over 1/4" thick that the ARV used in their multifilar coil but theirs used 1/4" copper rod surrounded by 1/8" of epoxy. I estimated that the ARV multifilar coil maxed out around 125,000 volts, this was a conservative estimate. Regardless in a space where nine 150kV 8mm wires would fit, twenty-five 30kV 5mm wires would fit. 9 * 150kV is 1,350kV. 25 * 30kV = 750kV. I decided that 150kV wire would be best with a voltage rating to construct the new overunity free energy alternator generators and to construct the anti-gravity, anti-inertia multifilar coil.

With this in mind I decided on using the highest voltage wire. On eBay the wire was only sold in short segments, 30 feet being the maximum. I figured I'd have Driver shoot the guys in China, who made my flyback transformers, an email and ask if they had any 150kV wire for sale and if so what lengths. It would be much more of a pain in the ass to wire up the main multifilar coil and alternator generator coils but I think it would reduce inertia and gravity more than using the low voltage ribbon cable, or medium voltage wire.

To power the multifilar coil I needed DC current like Tesla's bifilar coil. This left me with making a Cockcroft Walton generator, a voltage multiplier like the Marx generator, but it instead takes in AC current and outputs constant DC rather than taking in DC current and outputting pulsed DC like the Marx.

112

It would be a simple five stage CW generator using 30kV AC flyback transformers for input basically like the ones used in making the Marx generators. As stated earlier the multifilar coil's power depends on the voltage used, not the current, little current runs through a multifilar coil, so hazarding a guess a single 30kV 200 watt flyback transformer might be enough to power the anti-inertia coil and the alternator generator coils. If not I can always add additional 30kV flyback transformers to the input of the CW generators.

Chapter 60 – Things Get Cooking

Driver arrived today with the G10 dielectric sheets, high dielectric strength epoxy, copper plates, three compartment metal boxes, and a vacuum chamber. It was time to get started making the six Biefeld-Brown parallel plate capacitors.

I degassed the epoxy in the vacuum chamber. Without degassing there would be tiny air bubbles in the epoxy that would make it easy for the electricity to break through the epoxy. I degassed the epoxy in the vacuum chamber until bubbles stopped moving to the surface and the epoxy sat still.

I placed a sheet of G10 dielectric down at the bottom of the center compartment of the metal box leaving equal space on all sides in the metal box. I then poured a little epoxy on the G10 dielectric spreading it around like a thin layer of peanut butter. I placed the sheet of 1/2" thick copper plate on top of the G10 dielectric sheet. I pressed down as firmly as possible on the 1/2" thick copper sheet. I then moved to the next capacitor letting the epoxy dry on the first capacitor between the G10 and copper plate.

After completing the six capacitor bottom dielectric and copper plates I took a break letting the epoxy dry and cure.

I then fired up Hulu and watched more Stargate SG-1 episodes, by far the most accurate sci-fi show reflecting reality here on earth. Good aliens, bad aliens, and a secret space program visiting other worlds.

I find myself relating the most to the Daniel Jackson character, the non-military team member of SG-1. Of course he was an expert in language and I could barely speak any Spanish despite the five years of classes during high school and college. His mind was not a military mind, he wanted to help people, the aliens and humans he found on the various worlds they traveled to. Perhaps Samantha Carter the second in command, expert on technology and physics was more reflective of me. That would be a conceit, for my knowledge of physics is poor. I am more of a detective, reading evidence and others work to come to my conclusions. That said, I would recommend Stargate SG-1 to anyone who wanted to see our reality as it really is.

If I couldn't be Zephram Cochrane of Star Trek lore and be the first to discover and travel faster than light I could at least be the first civilian to use the technology and bring it into the popular reality, the popular consciousness.

I awoke the next day, the epoxy dried and cured. I now degassed more epoxy and when that was done, proceeded to add to the layers of the capacitors. Over the next few days I added layer by layer until I had six complete Brown capacitors G10 | Epoxy | Copper | Epoxy | G10 | Epoxy | Copper | Epoxy | G10.

The last thing to do now was degas more epoxy and fill up the center compartment of the metal boxes containing the capacitors to the top of the metal boxes. They should now mount securely to the flying car frame and not move around or vibrate.

I fired up Hulu and watched some Stargate Atlantis, an interesting show, not as good as SG-1 but entertaining. The worst decision they made was getting rid of Dr Weir at the end of season three. After that they had two more seasons one each with different leaders. Maybe they were trying to raise the ratings, I don't really know, but it hurt the show and what was a five season show could have been seven or ten if they had just left things alone. Enough of my griping.

What I liked the most about that show was the giant city ship Atlantis. If only I had the automation technology and raw materials to build it I could start my own country in international waters off the east coast of the U.S. Really just a pipe dream but a nice one, speaking of which I could really go for some cannabis.

Chapter 61 – Dropped Off the Face of the Earth

Bill Armstrong had no leads on the location of Robert Francis, he appeared to have dropped off the face of the earth. No visuals on any cameras throughout their entire hijacked network of cameras throughout the entire world, no credit or debit cards used, no phone calls or instant messages to his family, friends, and associates, no purchases of electronics matching his patterns, no flight, train or bus tickets, he was simply gone.

At least for the time being his work on forbidden technology prototypes was at the least delayed, it would take time to acquire the needed materials again, the money to buy them which would be extremely difficult for him to do if he was earning less than minimum wage under the table somewhere, and such purchases, as all purchases are now, would be monitored.

But that was of little importance to Armstrong's bosses, they wanted Robert Francis found and eliminated now, not tomorrow, not next week, now. If he was still out there he was a threat to Project Luddite and Homeworld Security and to all the politicians who were in the executive branch or who had been in the Gang of Eight in the multi-decade long technology cover-up. People of high political power were turning the screws on Armstrong, the pressure was mounting.

Once thing was certain to Bill Armstrong, Francis would mess up. All people make mistakes and all it would take was a simple mistake for Project Luddite to reacquire Francis and take him in. For the sake of Armstrong's job he hoped that was sooner rather than later.

Chapter 62 – Cabin Fever

As much of a recluse I was I needed to get out. 24/7 inside the factory was making me stir crazy. I wanted to go out, to a local bar, get soused and have a good time. But I have seen **Person of Interest**, I know what the government could be capable of: surveillance of everything all monitored by an AI. And unlike the characters in Person of Interest, I had no ID masking going on within the AI, unlike the characters in the show if there was an AI monitoring all cameras I would not appear under some false identity,

I would immediately be identified and the AI would task its human handlers with murdering me, all to prevent the release of technology they've been hiding for the better part of seven decades.

So there I stayed in the factory, in my solitary confinement, a prison of no escape. The Brown capacitors were completed. Time to build the six Marx generators. This time instead of using tungsten rods and slowly rounded over the edges into a ball, I bought tungsten balls with a blind hole, a hole that doesn't go all the way through the tungsten ball. Making the Marx generators was tedious. Lots of soldering with small components.

30kV 100pF ceramic capacitors littered my work area, along with small inductors, 30kV wire, and the tungsten balls. I slowly methodically soldered together the Marx generator stages one by one, choosing to solder them into completed Marx generators after each stage had been completed. A kind of assembly line process going on.

Finally with all the stages complete I started soldering the stages together. This was a little quicker and time seemed to fly by. It was also quite satisfying as I got to see my Marx generators starting to take shape.

With the fully assembled Marx generators complete, six positive generators, six negative generators for the six capacitors with one positive lead and one negative lead each I was finally ready to install them into the metal boxes and connect them to the 30kV flyback transformers and Brown capacitors. I had to attach them to the metal boxes in the inside and outside compartments next to the Brown capacitors.

My ability to focus is waning. Maybe I could ask driver for some alcohol or cannabis, though I imagine cannabis runs a risk I shouldn't take; being illegal in Switzerland and all.

Forced into sobriety, yikes. I never really considered myself an addict. Perhaps that is just denial. On the other hand I've been without cannabis or alcohol for a month and I'm not craving it. Not enough to risk blowing my anonymity. Paraphrasing Dr. Drew from Loveline with Adam Carolla and Dr. Drew, you are an addict if you continue to use drugs and alcohol inspite of escalating consequences. I could not have pot get in the way of my work on the flying car. The less potential heat on me the better, even if I had to go without on some of the things I enjoyed.

If driver could get it he could, if it was a risk, then forget it. I had a mission to complete, building the first real flying car, I wasn't about to let a little pot habit stop me.

On that note I continued my work on the GPS connected to the Raspberry Pi. I wanted to be able to enter a destination and have the system either fly there by itself or at least give me an arrow, pointing me in the direction of the destination so I could manually fly there.

It had to be accurate and efficient. I needed to fly in a direct line to the Super Bowl stadium not zig zag across America. I would fly as low to the water and ground as I could but I couldn't be sure that this would keep me safe and undetected.

I definitely needed an altimeter of some sort, one that would always keep me above the waves or trees, power lines, and skyscrapers. A normal altimeter would not be good enough. I had to scrape the ground and an altimeter doesn't tell me anything but the pressure outside the craft.

I would need some kind of ground scanning equipment to keep me above the treetops and buildings. I would be flying at near night, so no sun to help keep me safe, I would need some kind of scanning array to pickup tall objects and alert me or even alter course automatically. The NoIR cameras would help but while they increased the contrast of the picture with their lack of a filter on infrared radiation, they were no night vision cameras.

Outside help on this would be much appreciated. At the speeds I would be going I don't think night vision would be enough. I would be on top of the object before I had a chance to pull up and avoid the object.

After doing a little research on the web I came across radar altimeters which use radar pulses directed at the ground to determine how high above the ground the craft is. The main problem I see with this is either buying or building a radar altimeter and integrating it into my flying car's systems. I have no experience with either. Something tells me a radar altimeter is not cheap, I guess on the bright side Driver has not said anything about a budget.

The only other option I could see was downloading some topographic maps and ensuring I fly above the highest points, a risk for sure, the last thing I would want is to be detected by the U.S.' radar system, I had to fly below it for the mission to be a success.

However topographic maps would be the easiest to use and integrate with my systems. Something to look into.

Chapter 63 – Bob's Burgers

The once a week grocery delivery man arrived today. Finally some hamburger and bacon to make a nice cheeseburger on my new Foreman Grill. With the Foreman Grill it was so easy, set the temp, set the timer and when it beeps it's done. It had been too long since I had one of these. I could live off of bacon cheeseburgers with lettuce, tomato, sweet pickles and ketchup on a potato bun. So succulent and delicious.

That said I do have some issues with eating meat. They say pigs have the intelligence of a 2-3 year old, not sure about cows. I know humankind has been omnivores since forever and animals kill other animals all the time in the wild.

You could say I am enthusiastically looking forward to lab grown meat. It will become a reality and sooner than people think. Some won't be willing to eat it, its not really organic after all. But if it tastes the same and no animals have to die to make it, I am on-board.

There is of course also the environmental benefits as well, reduced methane gas going into the atmosphere from cattle flatulence reducing human caused climate change. Waterways will be less polluted by animal manure runoff.

Fish stocks around the world will start to rebuild from their near extinction due to over fishing. This will have a positive benefit for all the ocean's ecosystems.

To get on my high horse I think there is a real possibility that dolphins, killer whales, and elephants are as smart as we are. They have brains as big or bigger than our own. They just lack hands and opposable thumbs necessary to draw and write to make a readable language and then the tools necessary to then work with each other on humanoid mechanical and technological projects.

Heck, even Koko the gorilla could sign like eight hundred words and gorillas aren't much smarter than pigs.

All that said I do love bacon cheeseburgers.

Chapter 64 – Creating the Overunity Free Energy Generators

I decided that instead of three overunity free energy generators I would build six. I wanted to be completely positive that I had enough energy generation on-board to power all on-board systems with energy to spare.

The supplies for creating the alternator generators were brought in by Driver today.

12 - 10" PVC end caps

6 - 10" foot long PVC pipes

12 - 250 amp alternators

6 – 12V DC to 120V AC inverters

6 – Large spools of 150kV wire

12 – Copper bus bars

12 – 30kV AC flyback transformers

6 – 24 volt power supplies

1 – Tube of Locktite

Large assortment of diodes

Large package of 30kV ceramic capacitors

Long bolts

Mosfets

I started with building the Cockcroft Walton voltage multipliers. I decided I would build a full wave CW generator, their output is more reliable than a half wave CW generator. I started an assembly line process of building the individual stages in CW generators with capacitors and diodes.

After soldering up enough CW voltage multiplier stages I began soldering the stages together. This proceeded at a decent pace, it was nothing compared to the number of stages in the Marx generators that fed the Biefeld-Brown flat parallel plate capacitors.

Each CW full wave voltage multiplier has two AC inputs. For the inputs I used one 30kV AC 200 watt flyback transformer for each input. Powering the AC flyback transformers was a mosfet capacitor and diode combo that raised the AC voltage coming from the 12DC to 120V AC inverter to 170 volts.

With the CW voltage multipliers done I proceeded to build the PVC contained alternator generator combos. The alternators had the same four bolt method to hold the alternator together that the prototype I built in Connecticut had. It was easy enough drilling the holes in the PVC end caps and mounting the alternators to the end caps.

For six of the alternators I hacked the devices in order to apply current from the 24 volt power supplies to the three taps in the alternators to turn the alternators into motors with a low voltage applied to the rotor creating a magnetic field in the rotor.

Before mounting the PVC end caps to the PVC pipe I applied locktite to six of the alternator nuts to ensure the nuts would not come off.

I had to drill some holes in the PVC end caps and pipes which I would feed the two ends of each bifilar pancake coil wire through. The beginning of cable one connects to the end of cable two and the beginning of cable two connects to ground. The end of cable one connects to 150kV. I added two copper bus bars inside the PVC pipe. One bar would connect to ground, the beginnings of cable two. The other bar would connect the beginnings of cable one out past the end of the coil to the ends of cable two.

I then lined up the hex sockets to connect each alternator motor to alternator generator combo. With a little weight and wacks with a mallet I got the end-caps solidly on with the alternator motors now turning the alternator generators.

Now it was time to wrap the 150kV wire around the PVC where the alternator generators were. This would be tricky. With the 80 wire ribbon cable the cable wanted to naturally sit flat where they were wrapped around the PVC end cap. With the 150kV wire I would need some kind of plate to act as a guide in order to wire the bifilar pancake coil so that each turn of the cable sat properly on the cable turn below it.

If I were to create a plate out of plywood or something I could cut a hole so it would fit snugly on the end of the PVC end caps. From there I could wire each bifilar pancake coil one by one using the plate and then the bifilar pancake coils as guides wiring the rest of the coils until the entire alternator generator was surrounded by the multiple bifilar pancake coils creating a multifilar coil for each generator.

I wrote up the specs for the plywood guide plate and would give Driver the specs next week. Surely Driver could find a business to make it. For ease and speed I might just have Driver go to the local motorcycle shop and make the guide plate out of metal that they could cut with a plasma cutter.

Now it was just a waiting game, waiting for Driver to get the part design from me, waiting for Driver to get the part made at a local shop, waiting for driver to return with the part, so I could finally wire up the coils on the alternator generators.

With some free time I decided to crack open a few cold ones and fire up Hulu, watching some more Stargate SG-1. I was eager to finish the overunity free energy alternator generators but I just had to be patient. Maybe I would try some more meditating.

Chapter 65 – Homesick

It's been about a month now since I've been on the run.

A month without talking daily with my mom on the phone.

A month without hugging my father daily, seeing him alive and well.

A month without chatting daily with my friend Gary on AIM.

A month without seeing my brother and his girlfriend Amy.

A month without seeing my friends Steve and Mike.

A month without emailing my friend Heather.

A month without going out with friends and getting drunk and high.

A month without web browsing my usual haunts, slashdot.org, arstechnica.com, wired.com, newscientist.com, sciencedaily.com, abovetopsecret.com.

A month without Buffy the Vampire Slayer, Angel, Hercules, Xena, Star Trek The Next Generation, Star Trek Deep Space 9, Star Trek Voyager, and Star Trek Enterprise.

A month without anyone to talk to except short exchanges with Driver or the grocery deliverer.

This is far more difficult than I would have thought.

But it's worth it, giving the flying car to the earth: propellantless propulsion, anti-gravity, anti-inertia, and overunity free energy. These technologies will change the dynamics of the world irrevocably. The changes to this world that this technology will bring cannot be understated and on balance the positives will vastly outweigh the negatives.

One obvious benefit is greatly shortened commute times for the world's workers. Right now in America the average worker spends nine days a year commuting back and forth to work. Imagine the average commute of twenty six minutes reduced to about five minutes. Imagine a seven hour long flight to see distant relatives in another country reduced to less than half an hour. That is more time for family, friends, and hobbies.

Flying cars that were entirely automated would probably be a necessity but like self-driving cars they would open up transportation for all those who for one reason or another can't drive and dramatically reduce transportation deaths. Over 30,000 people each year in the U.S. die from traffic fatalities. With self-driving cars and self-flying cars this number will be massively reduced.

Besides without successfully completing the mission I will never get to go back home but if it is a success the powers that be will have no reason to go after me other than revenge. And since I am not outing anyone, who will there be to take revenge? I haven't burned an agency like Snowden did to the NSA. I'm just a civilian, a detective, not a whistle blower. All the knowledge I used was already freely available on the internet if you did enough digging and had a little luck in that search. Perhaps that's naive, they may still want to make an example of me, I guess I just hope I will be able to go back to my old life when this is all done.

Chapter 66 – Nose to the Grindstone

I finally got the throttle control wired through an Arduino connected to the pulse rate of the trigatrons on all of the three top Marx generators. Throttle at zero: no pulses; throttle at maximum: one hundred pulses a second.

Connecting the flight stick control to an Arduino to pulse the different capacitors depending on the direction the flight stick was being directed would be much more challenging. Pushing left or right on the flight stick would be used to roll the craft in either direction. For rolling left I would have to send voltage pulses to the top right Brown capacitor and the bottom left Brown capacitor. For rolling right I would do the opposite, send voltage pulses to the top left Brown capacitor and the bottom right Brown capacitor.

I also needed a cut-over switch so when I want an all stop and not move in any direction the system takes over and the flight stick and throttle are not used until the cut-over is disengaged. Landing the flying car should also be done without the flight stick and throttle, they would be too imprecise. I need very precise control when approaching a parking space to avoid trees, power lines, buildings, other parked cars and pedestrians.

I approach a place to land the flying car, I enter all stop and then slowly descend and maneuver into the parking space. Computer assisted parking like some vehicles have to parallel park a car would be a great asset here. It would be nice to make an automated landing system. Put the craft in hover mode over the parking space and turn on the landing autopilot having it slowly descend using the bottom facing camera to land within the parking space. A nice feature, something I might work on if I have the time.

Yes, I think a cut-over would be a good idea. A switch to switch between the flight stick and throttle flying mode and the trackball precise maneuvering flying mode. The switch should be easy enough to make, an electrical switch, maybe one of those cool flip the cover click switch types. The pulses to the capacitors would be switched between the Arduino controlling the pulses of the flight stick and throttle and the Arduino controlling the pulses connected to the trackball.

The trackball would control the movement of the craft in very small increments always going back into hover mode when the trackball stops moving. The trackball's left and right mouse buttons would be for controlling vertical assent and descent. With a ground facing camera on the bottom of the craft I could use it like a backup camera with projected lines that show where the craft will land and then slowly descend into the space.

The keyboard would be for entering a destination and with the GPS module and some software I could get a direction pointer to lead me to the destination, kind of like Star Wars Galaxies when a landmark was highlighted an arrow on the screen would show you which direction the landmark is. There are no roads, you hover on speeder bikes above the ground aiming your craft to make the navigation arrow point straight up, which is what I want for my flying car.

Chapter 67 – Jim Crow Laws Still in Effect, Just a Different Form

This is not the first time I have come across this information. In the 2000 Presidential election an investigative reporter named Greg Palast got a hold of a voter felon list. Voter felon laws disproportionately affect the democratic party as felons are more likely to vote Democrat than Republican. It is a cynical tactic to deprive Americans who have served their sentence from voting their conscience. In Florida it is illegal to vote if you have been convicted of a felony. Florida maintains a list of these felons so they cannot vote. It turned out that around 90,000 names on the list were non-felons. The vast majority of the people on the list were African American though.

It is well known that around 90% of African Americans vote Democrat. This bogus voter felon list cost Al Gore the Presidency in 2000. To make it all the more corrupt, Jeb Bush, the brother of

George W. Bush, was the governor of Florida at the time overseeing the Secretary of State of Florida whose responsibility among others was maintaining the voter felon list.

Flash forward to 2016, under the guise of removing duplicate voters from the registration rolls a list called Crosscheck was used in numerous battleground states. It by far contained Hispanic, African American, and Asian names. They removed people who had the same first and last name but different middle names. This disproportionately affected the Democrats as minorities tend to vote Democrat.

There were about 7 million names on this cross country voter list. About 2 million names were clearly different people with different middle names. Not one of the people on the list was arrested for voting twice. Voting twice is a felony and yet no one is prosecuted for it because it doesn't happen.

Furthermore many of the voting machines like in states such as Ohio have voter audit logs that can be enabled creating an image of each person's vote. This in effect creates a paper ballot that can be counted instead of relying on the totals the machines calculate which can be easily hacked.

None of the audit logs were turned on in states like Ohio and North Carolina making it impossible to determine if any voter hacking had occurred.

What is it with Republican politicians and their continuation of Jim Crow laws designed to prevent African Americans and other minorities from voting? They know these voters will vote for their opponent, the Democrats.

Finally, when will we get rid of the electoral college?

One man, one vote is the case for local, state and federal representatives with the exception of the Presidency. Al Gore and Hillary Clinton both won the popular vote in 2000 and 2016 yet we had a Republican President due to the electoral college. Clinton won the popular vote by over two million votes and yet was denied the Presidency.

Some people think the electoral college is important, that it prevents a few states with really large populations from getting to pick the President. What these people aren't saying but is nevertheless the reality of the situation is that they feel their votes should count for more than one vote and large population states should have their votes count for less than one vote. States are not monoliths, they are not a singular organism, they are composed of millions of people who are rightfully entitled to have their vote count as much as anyone else's in any other state.

We must insist on one man one vote, the end of the electoral college, along with the end of Jim Crow laws that exist to this day to deny votes to minorities to skew elections toward Republicans.

Chapter 68 – Coil Winding Time

Driver arrived today with the plate to mount to the PVC end caps to use as a guide for winding the coils on the PVC end caps and tubes.

I eagerly took to my task, the plate fit snug on the PVC end cap but that was perfect, it would act excellently as a guide for winding the coils.

I used the same number of turns in my multiple bifilar pancake coils as the ARV supposedly used in their coil loops according to Gordon Novel and the diagram in his book Supreme Cosmic Secret.

I cut up a bunch of equal length 150kV wires to make the bifilar pancake coils.

Winding the wire with the guide was easy, it just took some patience and attention to detail. The tricky part was feeding the beginnings of the bifilar pancake coil 150kV wire through the holes in the PVC, and from there, soldering them to their respective copper bus bars.

Once that was done, winding the coils went by quickly. I just kept the wire taut and snug firmly up against the guide plate. Once that first bifilar pancake coil was wound I proceeded to wind the next ones in the same fashion as the first with the exception of using the previous bifilar pancake coil as the guide. I completed the rest of the bifilar pancake coils in the same fashion

After I finished my first alternator generator I fired it up connecting my desktop PC, foreman grill and other electronics to the alternator generator. I was pulling about 2500 watts from the overunity free energy alternator generator. A nice step up from the 1500 watts pulled out by 300 volt ribbon cable I used in the prototype.

From there I proceeded to wire up the remaining five alternator generators and pressing the end caps onto the PVC pipe lining up the hex sockets so the alternator motors would deftly turn the alternator generators.

With all six alternator generators running I should have about 15,000 watts of electricity available to power the flying car. Plenty with enough to spare.

Chapter 69 – Knowledge is Power

All Seeing Eye was performing as expected. Terrorist threats were being caught before they happened. Violent crimes, murders and assaults were in some case prevented and others brought to justice after the fact thanks to constant omnipresent monitoring by ASE. The perpetrators were being brought to justice at record rates.

The NSA had to use a technique called **parallel construction** to keep the existence of ASE a secret from the public and the vast majority of Congress.

Parallel construction is a technique of using unlawful surveillance techniques to find a criminal and then calling in phony tips to give the police probable cause to search the criminal's home or vehicle for signs of criminality. The criminals were only found due to unconstitutional means which could not be used as evidence in a court of law, hence the use of parallel construction.

NSA's All Seeing Eye was even being used for nonviolent drug crimes, from low level dealers to high level kingpins. All it took was a little unconstitutional spying.

Monitor all conversations.

Look into the conversations between a drug dealer and his buyer.

Run a voice print identification procedure to identify the dealer and buyer.

Or

Pin point the source of the call. Use nearby cameras to catch the person on video, use facial recognition software to identify the person.

Then use parallel construction, have ASE call in fake phone tips giving police probable cause to investigate the person and arrest them.

Police were getting swamped with the increase of tips on their tip lines. To them it seemed everyone was turning on their friends and associates at record rates. Many were working overtime which if you are familiar with overtime for the police is both positive and negative. Working crazy hours is incredibly draining but the pay is outstanding.

The darknet drug markets were not any more secure than conventional drug deals. They too could be tracked by analyzing the bitcoin blockchain. The only protection afforded a drug user would be to launder your bitcoins through a tumbler that gives you different bitcoins than the ones you purchased with your debit or credit card along with a fee for using the service and hope that they did not keep any logs in case the government seizes their servers.

So far the darknet was not a priority but it would be. All Seeing Eye was correlating purchases of bitcoins with checks and credit cards and matching those coins to purchases from drug dealers. Drug dealers and drug markets on the darknet were being infected with firmware malware at high speed. With compromise of those PCs and servers it would be easy to correlate the bitcoin transactions and determine who purchased what.

We were awakening to a brave new world where privacy was gone and the state had knowledge of everything. Knowledge is power and those in charge of All Seeing Eye had power over everyone.

Chapter 70 – Strawberry Daiquiris

I have a sweet tooth, I am not ashamed to admit it. Growing up at family gatherings, holidays in the spring and summer, the adults would often make strawberry daiquiris for themselves and virgin ones for the kids.

Ever since then I have loved strawberry daiquiris. It had been months since I had one and I was getting a craving.

Grocery delivery was right on time today and in it he had strawberry daiquiri mix. One problem, I forgot to request a blender. I would tell Driver of my need for one when he stopped by tomorrow.

There is just something about them, strawberry flavor, tiny little blended ice pellets, sucking the mix down a straw. I didn't have them too often but I sure did enjoy them.

I guess its really just a smoothie, a strawberry smoothie. But at least in the U.S. you could never go out and buy a strawberry smoothie at the local Dunkin Donuts. They would have additional flavors in them or McDonalds would make it but carbonated.

Of course McDonalds did have vanilla shakes, another guilty pleasure of mine. They weren't as good as you'd find at an ice cream shop but they were good and consistent.

Some people would say that a strawberry daiquiri is a girlie drink implying that men who imbibe them are girlie. I say let your flag fly. If you like strawberry daiquiris or appletinis or whatever, be proud, own that part of yourself. Anyone who gives you grief is just trying to have fun, make a joke, or they are just being stupid.

Order up, give me a strawberry daiquiri.

Chapter 71 – MIA Assumed Dead

A couple months had gone by and there was still no sign of Robert Francis. Perhaps he died of exposure out in the wilderness. It would explain why All Seeing Eye has not found him.

Posts on the ARV, Biefeld-Brown effect, anti-gravity, anti-inertia, and overunity free energy have all but dropped off. No new messages from newcomers, or old comers using a new identity on the Above Top Secret honeypot nor the Reality Uncovered honeypot.

No contact with friends or family, something that would be very unlikely if he was still alive as just about all fugitives reach out at some point. Though if his family and friends think he is a terrorist that could be the reason why. There were still all points bulletins out for him but in all honestly All Seeing Eye would find Francis before local police and homeland security would.

Armstrong hoped he was dead. It would certainly simplify things and make his job easier. If he wasn't dead he had either picked up wilderness survival skills and is living off the land in some forest or someone is hiding him and doing a damn good job of it. If either these were the case Project Luddite might not have heard the last of Francis, a prospect that did not sit well with Armstrong.

Chapter 72 – Aborted Homopolar Generator

All Seeing Eye had put together a case against a man in India. He was working on a homopolar generator the likes of which Bruce DePalma and a nuclear engineer in India had done. He had visited sites on Bruce DePalma and the Indian nuclear engineer and was reading articles on homopolar generators including the proposed **Counter Rotating Homopolar Generator** on the **JASON** web site.

He had purchased a bunch of two foot diameter beryllium copper discs: an alloy of copper with a very high tensile strength which would be necessary in spinning copper discs at high speed; a large spool of copper wire presumably for making an electromagnetic coil, copper bars: for making a rotating cage of spinning copper discs inside a larger rotating cage of spinning copper discs; and a couple of high horsepower motors. He appeared to be building a counter rotating homopolar generator. Project Luddite sent a team into India to talk him out of his plans, giving him an offer he couldn't refuse. After the offer the man willingly gave the team his parts and swore to never work on it again, baffled as to how they could know what he was doing before he had built it or had told anybody about it.

Other than a blip here or there Project Luddite's days have been relatively quiet, most of the people they are monitoring have been quiet. Armstrong was sure the silence wouldn't keep but he was happy to have the situation well in control and handled. He could not have another garage tinkerer successfully producing a working prototype of any forbidden technology and with All Seeing Eye monitoring everyone and everything that was less likely than ever.

Chapter 73 – Deterioration

The North Korea situation was going from bad to worse. Somehow they were increasing the dielectric strength of the dielectric in their capacitors.

Homeworld Security has monitored several ballistic missile launches using Biefeld-Brown parallel plate capacitors by the North Korean state. While not particularly faster than a traditional ICBM they were far more reliable than previous conventional North Korean missiles.

Very shortly it was feared, that North Korea would have the capability to strike the U.S. with one of their Brown capacitor missiles, missiles with nuclear warheads.

Homeworld Security had the capability of shooting down their missiles but it would theoretically reveal their capabilities. Without an intervention in North Korea, they would simply make better, more durable, faster missiles. There would be an arms race, measure and countermeasure.

Homeworld Security was still deliberating on what should be done with the country. The U.S., U.K., And France wanted to destroy the country's leadership and extract their scientists. Russia wanted to destroy their leadership and kill the scientists feeling they had nothing to offer above what Russia's elite scientists already knew. China didn't want to lose their ally and alter the balance of power in their area of the world, or at least officially.

They were soon running out of time however and a North Korea with Brown capacitor ICBMs would alter the balance of power in the entire world. That was not something the majority of the Homeworld Security council could allow to come to pass. They would have to sweeten the pot for China to bring them on-board.

The U.S. was considering giving China a chemical formula for a higher strength dielectric than the ones China currently possessed. The U.S. had even better dielectrics in their inventory so they would not lose their edge to China with such a deal. Unfortunately the U.S. might have to go a step further and deliver one of their space cruisers to Chinese hands. That was the big poker chip, one they hoped they didn't have to add to the pot.

Chapter 74 – What the Hell Happened?

At a Halloween party many of Robert Francis' friends got together. Inevitably gossip started but the main question on everyone's mind was what did he do?

They heard the official story, that he was a terrorist that he and Emmanuel Goldstein had killed a bunch of people at a warehouse but it just didn't add up.

Where did he hear about these people?

How did he get there?

Why would he kill people when he has been non-violent?

Where did he go?

Did this have anything to do with his fringe science ideas?

There were no real answers only speculation.

So they did what they usually do, have a good time with friends, trying to stay in the moment and enjoy their lives. Alcohol was drunk, cannabis was enjoyed, merriment was had by all.

Project All Seeing Eye was there too. Listening to their conversations through their cellphones whose mics had been activated for eavesdropping. But there did not appear to be any answers in there.

They did not know where he was and neither did All Seeing Eye.

Chapter 75 – Homeworld Security's Work With the Greys

Homeworld Security has committed itself to defending Earth with all its forces. They were trying to build ships and man them as fast as possible. This wasn't easy for one nation to do secretly which is one of the reasons the U.S. expanded Homeworld Security to include the other permanent members of the U.N. Security Council. They needed the money, resources, and manpower.

In the past the U.S. relied on running the illegal drug trade throughout the world and funneling the money into their forbidden technology special access programs but this was no longer enough.

Earth's defensive technologies had been greatly enhanced with help from the Greys. Plasma beams, weaponized lasers, and shields were all imparted to humanity by the Greys in exchange for permission by our governments to take DNA samples of humans in an effort to create a hybrid Grey who could procreate.

The Greys had become sterile due to cloning and radiation damage to their DNA. They were a dying species and badly needed the infusion of fresh new DNA, DNA they could combine with their own to retain their powerful minds and keep their species alive.

Chapter 76 – Mounting the Marx Generators

With all Biefeld-Brown flat parallel plate capacitors mounted in the metal boxes it was now time to mount the Marx generators in the metal boxes and immerse them in transformer oil. I had to securely attach them while keeping them compact and encase the positive and negative leads in transformer oil to prevent any arcing and ensure the current goes into the Brown capacitors.

The Marx generators were already pretty compact but I decided to add high temperature PVC tube surrounding the tungsten spark gaps to help ensure that sparks go from one tungsten emitter sphere to the correct tungsten receiver sphere while keeping out any transformer oil ensuring a path for the electricity to travel within the Marx generator.

There were two Marx generators for each Brown capacitor one negative, one positive, delivering a -1MV and +1MV into the negative and positive plates of the capacitor.

The ARV had to be simpler than this. The cutout showed a bunch of tall cylinders around the base of the crew pod, maybe they were

Marx generators. Or maybe they used a Cockcroft Walton generator and had a kind of distributor cap where the electricity from the CW was dispersed by a rotating device that spent brief pulses to the Brown capacitors as it rotated and emitted electricity.

Regardless I was set on making the system as solid state as possible. Rotating parts lead to broken parts, especially if I was to try and make a rotating discharge system from scratch. The alternators in the energy generators were about as durable as you can get, designed to go hundreds of thousand conventional automobile miles without service.

I laid the Marx generators horizontally, the positive one in the outside compartment in the metal box of the Brown capacitor and the negative on on the inside compartment of the Brown capacitor metal box. From there I poured transformer oil to surround the Marx generators and prevent arcing within the Marx generators. I used transformer oil around the Marx generators rather than epoxy so that the Marx generators could easily be repaired if one of the components dies.

Unfortunately due to suspected satellites capable of detecting a Brown capacitor signature I could not and would not test the flying car until Super Bowl Sunday. I know the Marx generators work, that was all tested before with a high speed camera able to see the voltage pulses.

The Brown capacitors however were an unknown. I wouldn't know if they had air bubbles or shorts in them till one fateful Sunday.

Chapter 77 – Pattern Match Detected

All Seeing Eye reported to its handlers a grocery shopping pattern match, detected through a compromised database at a grocery store, with Robert Francis' past purchases. Specifically hamburger, bacon, cheese, tomato, lettuce, sweet pickles and potato rolls.

There were many people purchasing the same things but this one stood out, it was in Switzerland, and it was a small purchase which made All Seeing Eye report on it, it was not the smorgasbord of a traditional Swiss cuisine.

It could be nothing and All Seeing Eye rated it a vague match. Bill Armstrong having no leads decided to task a team with monitoring the target. All ready recordings of his cellphone conversations were being poured over by humans to determine what he buys, who he calls, where he goes. Theoretically Robert Francis could be the target and was using a voice modulator during his phone calls avoiding voice pattern recognition algorithms.

It was a flimsy lead but the only one they have had in months.

The team dispatched to look into this pattern arrived in Switzerland and started human monitoring of his calls. The target was not Robert Francis but a local Swiss man. They decided they would monitor his travels, he kept a cellphone with him, like most of the rest of the western world, at all times. So far though it looked like a simple coincidence and there was no evidence pointing to him working with Robert Francis, never mind how Francis would have met the man or received his help.

The Swiss man was of course the grocery and parts deliverer to Robert Francis but Project Luddite did not yet know that. He never carried his cellphone on him when traveling to the abandoned plastics factory but if the Project Luddite team planted a GPS tracker on his car, all could be lost.

Chapter 78 – North Korea Nuclear Detonation

North Korea continued to advance in its dielectrics. The latest test involved detonating a nuclear weapon over the Atlantic Ocean. Their Biefeld-Brown flat parallel plate capacitor missiles were performing better than expected. Better than the U.S. and the rest of the council had anticipated.

A few more tests and North Korea would have nuclear strike capabilities across the continental United States. Or at the least they could detonate one of their nuclear weapons high up in the atmosphere over the United States triggering an EMP that could destroy all modern electronics in the country. Such an action would obviously turn the U.S. into a third world country. This threat could not be tolerated.

It was time to bring China into the fold. The U.S. offered the higher strength dielectric but China balked. The U.S. was up against a brick wall. It could not tolerate a North Korean regime and their bombastic attitudes towards the U.S. government combined with weapons that could, if not intercepted, destroy the American way of life as we know it. The U.S. would have to pay off, bribe, China and bring the council into unanimous agreement.

The U.S. member of the Homeworld Security council gave in and offered to give China one of its latest space ships. A cruiser with shields, lasers, and a fast Brown capacitor drive. This ship was more advanced than anything China had in their arsenal. The U.S. would still retain a significant tactical advantage having superior weapons, shields, and speed but it would make China the number three power amongst the five permanent members of the Homeworld Security Council, as far as forbidden technology goes.

Chapter 79 – Playing Some Bridge Commander

I decided to take a break from my work writing code for the GPS system. I didn't have the CD with me but there are always file sharing sites. I downloaded Bridge Commander and an add-on Quincentennial-Mod, a Bridge Commander mod that has five eras of Star Trek and all the ships and adversaries from those times.

The Quincentennial-Mod was 3.75GB, about 8 times the size of the original game. The graphics were outstanding, far better than the original game.

My favorite ship was the Federation's Defiant class as seen in Star Trek Deep Space 9. The craft has strong shields which are even stronger when emergency power is directed to the shields. It had ablative armor which helped keep systems protected and running when the shields were getting weak. It's pulse phasers can destroy a Dominion Attack Ship in one volley and the quantum torpedoes packed a heck of a punch. Other than the Borg cube there there was no ship I could not destroy with the Defiant.

Another one of my favorite craft was the Delta Flyer from Star Trek Voyager, probably because it was small but powerful, and very very fast. It took a lot of skill to fly the craft, torpedoes and pulse weapons had to be avoided to stay alive. Against ships with pulse fire weapons like most of the Klingon ships or the Federation's Defiant class it was cake. Just outmaneuver them with the high speed and maneuverability, stay on the enemy ships' belly targeting the warp core.

They didn't stand a chance.

Other ships with beam weapons were a lot more tricky for the Delta Flyer. The only real tactic is to stay in a ship's blind spot where they can't hit you or only have one beam weapon on that area of the ship rather than several. Take out the beam weapon, then target the warp core.

I was a beast with both ships. Even the Dominion ship from the Star Trek DS9 episode Red Squad was no match for me. First target the impulse engines to reduce its considerable maneuverability and speed, then target the sensor array blinding them.

Just about every ship has a weak point somewhere, just gotta know what it is and target it.

I guess that is what I was doing with my Super Bowl plan. Landing the ship at the 50 yard line during the most watched televised event in the world, it would reach millions upon millions.

A UFO could land on the White House lawn and be covered up with disinformation but the Super Bowl, that was a whole other level.

Same goes with spoofing the top ten most pirated shows: Game of Thrones, The Walking Dead, The Big Bang Theory, Arrow, The Flash, Mr Robot, Vikings, Supergirl, The Blacklist, and Suits.

Millions upon millions of people download those episodes. Spoofing such episodes by putting in my Forbidden Technology documentary would reach millions more.

There would be no putting the toothpaste back in the tube, no manner of disinformation or cover-ups would work and keep their forbidden technology secrets hidden.

I would have to be cautious with the show spoofing. It might not take long for the authorities to find out what I was doing, find my location, and work to shut it all down. I would have to start seeding the torrents right before I left for the Super Bowl.

Hundreds maybe thousands of videos about the Super Bowl landing would hit the torrent sites and Youtube just as people were viewing the Forbidden Technology documentary. There would be no putting the genie back in the bottle. No stopping the ensuing momentum. This world would see a brand new day.

Now I just have to get back to work.

Chapter 80 – Working on the GPS

The Raspberry Pi computers support wide variety of peripherals from cellphone data boards, to breakout boards to control industrial servo motors, to GPS modules.

The conventional GPS software would not work for my cause so I would have to write my own. There were gigabytes of maps of the United States available but the GPS software that uses them gives turn by turn directions, a popular feature on modern GPS devices. I however needed a directional arrow to appear on the screen, not turn by turn directions. I would be flying above roads, I would have no need for turn by turn functionality.

I have to enter a destination and then based on my location an arrow appear on the screen so I can manually steer towards the direction of the arrow until the arrow is pointing straight forward and then open up the throttle with a report on the screen of distance to destination and maybe even a time to destination at present speed.

An even better feature would be to enter a destination and hit "Go" causing the flying car to steer towards the destination and then go at maximum speed for a time until I had reached the destination then putting the vehicle back into manual mode for landing.

Unfortunately I didn't have the ability to do much testing before launch day. If I did I would try to incorporate this computer controlled flight into my vehicle but with limited programming knowledge and limited time, a simple arrow will be all I will focus on for this component of the flying car.

GPSD a Linux GPS program communicates with the GPS hardware attached to the Raspberry Pi. Many programmers use C or Python, or a combination of both to communicate with GPSD. Python was well supported on the Raspberry Pi so I decided to go with Python, a language I was not familiar with but I was not familiar with C either.

I just needed a simple Python app to give me an arrow, distance, and time to arrival by communicating with GPSD.

Time to get cracking reading the documentation of GPSD and Python. I had to get the directional arrow and other features working.

Chapter 81 – Arrow Overlay Complete

Work on the arrow overlay for the GPS was finally done. I entered a destination and the arrow overlay pops right up on the navigation screen aimed at the destination along with a distance to destination in kilometers. Rotating the GPS would alter the arrow overlay until it was pointed at the destination and the arrow overlay would point straight up on the display.

Another good feature to add would be having an X marks the spot on my flight monitors showing me an X over the destination when I arrive at my destination. It shouldn't be much harder to program than the arrow overlay and will give me one more piece of information to help me navigate to my destination.

A really cool feature would be to have parking spaces identified by the camera software and highlighted on the ground over the live feed. This is not a necessary feature but would be a really nice tool for quickly spotting parking spaces so I can go land in one.

I can only imagine one day the technology will exist to show all parking spaces highlighted on the screen and then click on the touchscreen the empty parking space and have the flying car land in it automatically. That however is beyond my current abilities, I wouldn't even know where to start. Perhaps if I have time before my first launch on Super Bowl Sunday I will try to add this functionality into the vehicle.

Since the canopy would be covered in aluminum plate painted with black lead paint I would be using cameras to feed my internal displays.

I was originally thinking of purchasing an off the shelf backup camera kit but since I was using standard cameras for the normal front facing flight mode it really wouldn't take much more effort to use another one of those cameras on the bottom of the craft.

Then I just use an HDMI switch to switch from front view to bottom view when landing the craft.

Chapter 82 – Citizens Dividend

Little did I know the extent of the NSA's All Seeing Eye program though I had my suspicions. One major issue with advancing AI is the smarter AI gets the more jobs it will eliminate. Sure some jobs will be created but not nearly as many as are lost.

Where will this leave humanity?

We have already seen the profits due to increased productivity go to the top 1% over the past several decades, why would things be any different when the productivity is due to AI rather than humans?

There will always be the attitude among some that those who aren't working are lazy and don't want to work. This attitude would leave ever increasing proportions of the population out of a job and with no means to provide for themselves.

Some politicians have raised the idea of a universal basic income. This would merely give people a subsistence level of existence, constantly worrying about paying the bills, being able to afford to put food on the table, able to consume only the bare minimum.

I think we need to go further than a UBI, I think a **Citizens Dividend** is necessary.

A citizens dividend takes the view that the natural resources of the planet belong to all of us rather than to groups who can afford to buy a mine for pennies on the dollar from a crooked government or from the first person to arrive at a new location.

Soon we will have space mining. Do those resources belong to the corporation that got there first or do they rightfully belong to all of us?

A citizens dividend would give all humanity payments for the resources that are extracted and sold. It was Thomas Paine who stated:

Men did not make the earth. It is the value of improvements only, and not the earth itself, that is individual property. Every proprietor owes to the community a ground rent for the land which he holds.

In the future it will be an AI system, thoroughly automated, that will make the improvements on the earth. Should not the spoils be given to all rather than the top 1%?

A future without a citizens dividend is a future where all humanity but the top 1% are reduced to barely getting by with no money to buy resources of their own, no ability to create with those resources. The top 1% will have all the natural resources and they will just as soon build things with those resources while leaving the rest of humanity plugged into some sort of digital matrix so the masses consume next to nothing but digital information and an IV drip while the top 1% own the whole planet, the whole solar system, everything.

We can't allow this to happen. We could use a Universal Basic Income, we need a Citizen's Dividend.

Mining for example is already automated to an extent. When the entire mining and refining process is automated by AI what need do we have for a corporation to do it while they take their cut of the profits? The lion-share going to those at the top of those corporations?

Patents expire, there is no reason that once the patents on automated mining and refining technology expire that with them in the public domain that government does not come in and run the mining and refining process all automated with all the profits going to all humanity instead of the top 1%.

If we the 99% do not fight for these programs we will be destitute while the top 1% lives like kings.

Our future is one in which machines make machines, machines maintain machines, and machines work for humanity. Do we want the productivity gains and profits to go to the top 1% or when these patents expire for the productivity and profit gains to go to all humanity?

Lastly resource wars would be a thing of the past. When a country gets the resources of a country it conquers, those resources go to the top 1% giving the top 1% an incentive to conquer other countries. When the leaders of a country and their top 1% financial backers no longer get the spoils of war, what incentive do they have for conquering a country? When the resources go to all the people divided equally, what incentive is there to conquer a country for their resources?

Alaska already does on a limited scale what I am recommending. Alaska gives money to every citizen for the oil that is extracted there. Is it a perfect system? No, the money given to each citizen for the oil extracted is not enough, more should go to the citizenry, less to the oil companies. But it does shine a light into what is possible, into what should be done country wide, world wide, for all the resources that are extracted.

We all will have to fight for it but this is the most equitable solution and one that should come to pass, if enough people are willing to protest for their share, it will come to pass.

Chapter 83 – The Partisan Politicization of Human Caused Climate Change

I am truly baffled that the next President of the United States, Donald Trump, does not believe human caused climate change is real and has appointed a fossil fuel pushing climate denier to his EPA transition team.

The vast majority of climate scientists throughout the world state that the evidence, the facts, show that humankind is causing climate change with our CO_2 emissions. The question for them has been how much of a change will we see?

Parts of Florida, NYC, Boston, and many points along the east coast will be under water if our CO_2 emissions continue on the current path.

When asked if "scientists believe in human caused climate change" a large majority of the country says yes. If the question is changed to "do you believe in human caused climate change" the country splits down the middle with Democrats largely believing in human caused climate change and Republicans disbelieving in human caused climate change.

How is this so? Why do Republicans disbelieve the scientific community?

Some say religion, that more conservative religious folk believe that God will ensure that the planet does not bury cities under a rising ocean or that such an event will bring us closer to Jesus' return.

This however does not explain why conservatives and liberals in other countries both believe in human caused climate change.

The only thing that makes sense to me is partisan politicization. According to studies partisanship is the highest its been in fifty years in the United States. Upwards of 40% of people are afraid of the opposition party leading the country.

In a sense the Republican coaches and team state there is no human caused climate change and their fans who vote for them take on those beliefs as their own completely unwilling to listen to Democrats who state we are changing our climate.

Whatever the cause, the world is spinning out of balance, species are dying at unprecedented rates, depending on how fast the Antarctic and Greenland ice sheets melt sea levels will rise slowly to quickly depending on how conservative the estimate is. In many cities the average number of days above 90 degrees would double by 2100.

And we have a President talking about using more coal, reviving the coal industry. Coal is the biggest producer of CO2 out of all the fossil fuels. It is also the dirtiest, spewing toxic chemicals into the air causing more deaths than nuclear power ever did.

I used to be a single issue voter, will they legalize cannabis and the rest of the drugs. There was a selfish tone to that vote considering I used cannabis. Now my single issue vote revolves around climate change. Does the candidate believe in human caused climate change? What are they willing to do to stop it and put the world back into balance? If they both are eager to tackle climate change then awesome I have a real choice to make at that point.

Human caused climate change is the single biggest issue facing the world and we are looking at a President, Donald Trump, who doesn't even believe it exists.

Chapter 84 – Camera Visual System

I decided that like the ARV I would use cameras mounted at different places on the craft and have them live feed into monitors in the cockpit rather than use a glass or plastic canopy which would be really expensive and difficult to build.

When the craft is flying straight one main camera will be aimed directly forward mounted on the top tip of the canopy. Another camera aimed up to see above me. A camera aimed below to see below me. And two cameras one facing left the other right to see out the sides of the craft.

I was originally going to buy an off the shelf backup camera kit that I would use to see the parking space I would descend in when landing the craft.

However a normal camera like the rest would be fine. I could simply have an HDMI switch to switch between the back facing camera and the front facing one on the main monitor.

I could opt for a VR helmet but frankly I am use to computer monitors, I use them throughout the day, I use them in video games, first person games, Bridge Commander, etc. It would also be complicated stitching the cameras together to paint a smooth picture to the VR helmet when looking around.

The Raspberry Pi has a camera model with no infrared filter for $30 which should be a little better during the dark and can feed live video into the Pi at 1080p @ 30fps or 720p @ 60fps.

Then I just put in one 1080p HDMI 23" Asus for the main screen. It will be surrounded by four 18.5" Asus 720p DVI monitors that I will use a converter since DVI is compatible with HDMI, along with an HDMI switch for the main monitor to select between the forward or landing camera.

I'm not footing the bill but six Raspberry Pi 3s and six camera modules are only $420.00, the monitors come to $460.00, $880.00 for my entire visual system, not bad. Something tells me the ARV's vision system costed orders of magnitude more money.

This did bring me to a problem, what would I do with the GPS X marks the destination and arrow overlay to put me in the direction of my destination. Currently a GPS map displayed on the monitor but that wasn't really useful for a flying craft. Far more useful would be to have the arrow overlay on the main monitor on top of the video feed from the camera.

Adding an X marks the spot overlay when near the destination on the main monitors video feed would also be the best option.

Somehow I had to use GPS but ditch the maps turn by turn window. I would need to make a custom program to create the video feed overlays tapping into the GPS through the Linux GPSD program's root protocols designing my own interface.

The video on the main monitor would have to act as a background because I would also need an overlay to enter in the destination address to then give me the arrow, distance to destination, minutes remaining.

More work to do.

Chapter 85 – Still at Large

The team based out of the U.S. embassy in Switzerland had been tracking the Swiss man Driver with the similar food purchases all week and he did not lead them to Robert Francis.

Just as the team was going to give up on this suspect, All Seeing Eye captured his vehicle in the city, his cellphone GPS was showing him at home. Either he forgot his cellphone or he left it home on purpose. Either way All Seeing Eye reported it to the team tracking the Swiss man.

The cameras were light in Switzerland, All Seeing Eye could not tell where he went just that he traveled through the city center of St Gallen. The Project Luddite team would have to go a step further and place a GPS tracker on the car so they could see where he went if he left his cellphone at home again.

Driver arrived at the plastics factory with the weekly groceries and set them down near the refrigerator.

I gave Driver my purchase list of monitors, raspberry pi kits, camera modules, HDMI cables, DVI to HDMI adapters. I gave a design for the monitor mounting bracket to Driver on a USB stick to have welded together at the motorcycle shop. Another part I designed on FreeCAD.

"Thanks, I'll see you next week."

I unpacked the groceries and made myself a delicious bacon cheeseburger.

Driver returned to his house in St Gallen, he would deliver the USB stick to the motorcycle shop on Monday when they were open. He parked his car and went inside.

One member of the Project Luddite team stood guard watching the movements of the Swiss man in his home while the other member planted the GPS tracking device under the rear bumper.

No fuss, this GPS tracker would tell the team exactly where the vehicle is at all times in real time.

Monday morning came and Driver delivered the monitor mount schematic to the local motorcycle shop. It wasn't really in their wheelhouse but they were glad to take the job it was honest work.

The part would be ready by Friday.

Chapter 86 - Tensions Flaring on the Korean Peninsula

North Korea was not happy with China's apparent reversal in support of the North Korean nuclear program. China's about face left North Korea increasingly isolated. With virtually no support and their backs up against a wall North Korea was in danger of lashing out militarily against South Korea and the United States.

The U.N. Security Council passed a unanimous resolution demanding the unconditional dismantlement of North Korea' nuclear program, the exportation of all enhanced and raw uranium.

Some of the North Korean military leadership called for all out war and to attempt to destroy the United States. Saner heads prevailed though as they knew they would not survive a retaliatory attack by the U.S.

With North Korea facing a war on all sides or the dismantling of their nuclear program they finally acquiesced. North Korea stated they would abide by the resolution and dismantle their nuclear program.

There was still plenty of red tape to go through, meetings and inspection agreements to be made.

But it looked like a nuclear North Korea would finally be a thing of the past.

In exchange for this move by North Korea, sanctions against the regime would be lifted in stages as they proved to the world that their nuclear program's pieces were being taken apart.

Furthermore a peace process would be established to end the state of war between North Korea and South Korea, each respecting the other's right to exist in a two state solution.

Chapter 87 – Propulsion and Navigation Systems Complete

All the software had been written for the navigation overlays. The programs screen was transparent and would allow the video feed to underlay it showing navigational elements on top.

The software running on the Arduinos controlled Marx generators was complete. The flight stick and throttle had complete control in manual mode, and the keyboard and trackball had control in landing or taking off mode when it was activated.

The only system left now was life support. A ship traveling fast enough to get from one side of the world to another in an hour couldn't have ordinary air vents to feed the cockpit with air. If air were to enter vents in the craft it would heat up and burn up at the speeds the flying car was traveling at. Never mind that the field around the craft from the multifilar coil or Brown capacitors might keep air away from the hull as UFOs are seen moving extremely fast and yet not heat up due to friction from the atmosphere therefore no air would enter a vent even if there was one. The ARV had no vents, it had a series of oxygen tanks but of course it was built for outer space.

I had no means of testing the ship in a vacuum to ensure that all panels and seams were fully sealed and would not leak even in the vacuum of space. Nor that the canopy when closed would be air tight either. The seals in the flying car should be good enough however for normal flight through the air since I would not be cruising at altitudes near the vacuum of space, never mind that I would try to fly very low to avoid the world's radar systems so no one would see me coming, no one would see that my course was direct line straight for for Levi's stadium in California.

Unfortunately I know next to nothing about life support systems, even down to scuba tanks. Off to Wikipedia. Spacecraft and space stations use carbon scrubbers to keep the carbon dioxide levels in check and ensure the CO_2 levels on board stay below certain thresholds. Too much CO_2 in the air and you begin to suffocate even if there is enough oxygen in the air. Definitely something I wanted to avoid.

It looks like I need a CO_2 scrubber of some kind along with an oxygen tank or two like in the ARV to slowly release O_2 into the air to replace the O_2 absorbed in my lungs.

An off the shelf re-breather for scuba diving would work albeit be really expensive, far more expensive than all the rest of the parts in my flying car. Of course I don't have to pay for it but still. It didn't seem like a very efficient use of my resources. I would also have to wear a breathing mask if I used an off the shelf scuba diving re-breather. I would prefer to just breath in recycled air in the cockpit cabin and not use a breathing mask.

I have a lot of research to do, I never even thought about this component of the flying car. My whole focus had been on the propellantless propulsion technology with minor interest in overunity free energy. I guess on the bright side carbon scrubbers are known technology so no need to reinvent the wheel here. Although to be fair I wasn't reinventing the wheel, like a good detective I followed the evidence, the facts, I didn't invent or discover anything.

Chapter 88 – Constant Warfare and Empire Building

We have been in a state of war with weak countries of the world for far longer than the 9/11 attacks. The common denominator is virtually always about money and resources or the boogeyman of communism. They have something we want and we overthrow their governments to get it throwing democracy to the wolves.

Iran

In 1953 the U.S. government in Operation Ajax helped overthrow the democratically elected government of Prime Minister Mohammad Mosaddegh after Mosaddegh nationalized the Iranian oil fields taking control of them from the hands of the Anglo-Iranian Oil Company.

In August 2013 the CIA admitted that it both planned and executed the coup, including bribing Iranian politicians, security, and army officials.

The CIA installed the Shah of Iran who led a brutal dictatorship in the country until 1979 when he was overthrown during the Iranian Revolution. Iran has been on the U.S.' shit list ever since.

Guatemala

In 1954 the U.S. government's CIA (Central Intelligence Agency) helped overthrow the democratically elected left-wing government of President Jacobo Arbenz in a coup d'etat and ended the Guatemalan Revolution. The code name for the coup was Operation PBSUCCESS. In Arbenz's place a military dictatorship was installed led by Carlos Castillo Armas.

The main reasons for this coup led by the U.S. were the labor reforms such as minimum wage laws and the land reform which granted land to peasants affecting the profits of the U.S. company United Fruit Company.

Guatemala led by Carlos Castillo Armas banned all political parties, tortured and imprisoned political opponents, and reversed the social reforms of the Guatemalan Revolution. U.S. backed dictatorships lasted in Guatemala for the next 42 years leading to a civil war.

Iraq

In 1963 the U.S. government's CIA supported the Ba'ath Party's overthrow of the Iraqi Prime Minister Abdul Karim Qassem who was threatening American and British oil interests in Iraq. Saddam Hussein became the new dictator of Iraq supported by the U.S. as the CIA recruited him to kill the Prime Minister.

Vietnam

In 1964 the Gulf of Tonkin incident also known as the USS Maddox incident occurred. It supposedly involved two confrontations involving North Vietnam and the United States. Supposedly the USS Maddox had been attacked by North Vietnamese torpedo boats.

This was the reason Lyndon Johnson used to wage war against North Vietnam when Congress passed the Gulf of Tonkin Resolution.

France had been occupying Vietnam for many years and the U.S. took over with this Gulf of Tonkin incident to prevent an independent government of Vietnam taking over as it had Communist leanings

Decades later it was revealed that the second confrontation with North Vietnam in the Gulf of Tonkin never occurred and in the first confrontation the U.S. fired first. North Vietnam had not attacked the U.S. at all.

Three to four millions Vietnamese died in the Vietnam War thanks to the attacks on the U.S. naval vessel Maddox that never occurred. The real motive appeared to be preventing a communist regime from rising in Vietnam.

Cambodia

In 1969 the U.S. bombed Cambodia, a neighboring country to Vietnam because some North Vietnamese troops would base their operations along the border of the two countries which Cambodia tolerated.

Half a million Cambodians died during these U.S. bombing campaigns directed by President Nixon. Two million Cambodians died when the brutal Pol Pot took control of Cambodia but this was considered the cost of doing business to the U.S. as Pol Pot was considered any enemy by the North Vietnamese. Henry Kissinger is quoted saying. "You should tell the Cambodians that we will be friends with them. They are murderous thugs, but we won't let that stand in the way. We are prepared to improve relations with them."

Chile

In 1973 the U.S. government waged economic warfare against the country of Chile in a successful attempt to oust socialist President Salvador Allende. Chile had been a shining symbol of democracy in South America with decades of democratic elections.

The military that overthrew Allende's Popular Unity government abolished all political activity in Chile and repressed left-wing movements with Augusto Pinochet the army chief ultimately rising to power. The U.S. government which helped drive out Allende quickly recognized the military dictatorship which lasted until 1988.

Iran-Iraq War

In 1980 the countries of Iran and Iraq went to war following a long history of border disputes and fears that the Iranian Revolution in 1979 would inspire Iraqis to rebel against their own government.

The U.S. supported Iraq's unprovoked attack of Iran due to the people of Iran overthrowing the U.S. backed dictator, the Shah of Iran. The U.S. provided biological and chemical weaponry for the Iraqis which were used on Iran along with $40 billion in loans to help Iraq win the war.

The U.N. Security Council even issued a resolution condemning the use of chemical weapons in violation of the Geneva Protocol of 1925. The only member of the council to vote against this resolution was the United States and with their veto power, they torpedoed the resolution.

Gulf War II

In March 2002 George W Bush was reported saying to Condaleeza Rice and three senators, "Fuck Saddam, we're taking him out." A full year before we invaded the country. Bush had already made up his mind on invading Iraq before any intelligence on Iraqi WMD was analyzed.

Furthermore the National Intelligence Estimate on Iraq which was classified painted a dramatically different picture than the summary of the NIE. Very few congressmen read the actual report which stated that despite suspicions, there was no proof Iraq had WMD.

When Joe Wilson a former ambassador was asked to look into the Iraqi purchases of uranium yellow cake rumors and found nothing he wrote an article for public consumption to dispel the rumors. In retaliation the Bush administration outed his wife a CIA agent named Valerie Plame whose undercover work involved counter-proliferation of WMD threatening her work and the work of her colleagues and associates.

War in Afghanistan

After determining that Osama Bin Laden had been the architect of the 9/11 hijackings and attacks on the World Trade Center and Pentagon we gave the Taliban leaders who had been eradicating poppy crops (used in the making of opium and heroin) the chance to turnover OBL. They wanted proof of OBL's involvement.

The U.S. refused to provide any proof to the Taliban of OBL's involvement and invaded the country. Soon after poppy crops were springing up throughout Afghanistan and U.S. soldiers were even guarding some of the crops. Afghanistan is once again a major supplier of heroin throughout the world.

Coup in Venezuela

In 2003 the democratically elected leader of Venezuela, Hugo Chavez, was briefly ousted in a coup supported by the U.S. At the time while the coup leaders were in power Bush was quoted saying that the coup was "democracy in action".

Luckily for Chavez he had supporters in the military who captured the coup plotters and forced them to reinstate Chavez as leader of Venezuela. Chavez had partially nationalized oil fields in Venezuela some of which were owned or partially owned by American oil companies like Exxonmobil.

A few years later Chavez came down with cancer and died. (Was it by a cancer weapon like the one used on Steven Greer?).

Since then Venezuela has been under economic warfare by the United States with their currency being practically worthless and falling oil prices have devastated the country, the profits of which had been used for many social programs in the country.

Chapter 89 – Building the Life Support System

From what I could tell about re-breather systems for divers I believe I can create a custom unit for far less than what a re-breather diving rig would normally cost.

One component is the carbon scrubber material. That material is available for a reasonable price if I ditch the rest of the scuba diving re-breather gear. I would merely need a container of the carbon scrubber material, a variety of which could be used. I could use the material in my own custom made design, with an intake and exhaust fan circulating the air of the cabin through the container of carbon scrubber material to remove the CO_2 from the air.

I would need a pure oxygen tank or two, basically depending on what would fit in my flying car along with a sensor attached to the oxygen tank valves that would release a small amount of O_2 into the cabin and keep the O_2 at a steady level equivalent to sea level. Plenty good enough for a normal sober experience unlike breathing in pure oxygen, which if used would probably lead to a combustible fire in the cockpit as had happened in NASA's Apollo 1 accident.

I could put the O_2 tank on the right side of the flying car against the cabin and the carbon scrubber container on the left side of the flying car. A couple simple low rpm, low noise 120mm Panaflo computer fans, like I used in my marijuana grow closet to pull cooler air through the hot, high wattage lights, would do the trick to blow the cockpit cabin air through the scrubber and remove the CO_2 in the air.

Chapter 90 – GPS Transponder

Driver was a professional, he had done this type of work, keeping people in safe houses, for a long time. He was always meticulous in doing his job, not sloppy, not shoddy.

Every day when he would get into his car he would turn on his bug detector to scan for bugs like GPS transponders. On this fateful day his bug detector went off.

Someone had planted a tracker on his vehicle. Knowing that he was being monitored and probably due to his current charge. He went along with his schedule like normal, not wanting to alert those who were monitoring him that he was onto them.

Robert Francis was no longer safe in Switzerland. Sooner or later they would find him at the plastics factory, his prototype flying car destroyed, and his chance to reveal the technology to the world gone along with his life.

Driver would go about his business for the next few days as normal as possible.

On Sunday when it was time to make his scheduled delivery to Francis he would have to take him to a new safehouse with a new ally taking care of his needs.

Chapter 91 – The Escape

Driver pulled up to the plastics factory in his usual car. He had removed the GPS transponder attached to the inside of the bumper and left his cellphone at home as per usual. If the traffic cameras had caught him the team that placed the GPS transponder would know he left and might be looking for him. He had to get Francis to the new safehouse as soon as possible.

He proceeded into the factory. He told Francis about the tracker.

"Take everything! The computers, the software, the USB sticks, your prototype flying car and its parts. Help me load it into the back of the container truck that's parked at the dock."

"We're headed to Amsterdam. I have an associate there that will set you up with a lab in the city and take care of your needs."

We packed up all my gear, the flying car, the miscellaneous parts all into the container truck. There was a GPS in the truck. Driver entered the destination.

"You're gonna have to take this trip on your own. They will be looking for me. They probably know I found the GPS transponder and will be watching me like a hawk. Just follow the GPS directions and it will take you to your knew handler. Get going, you must leave immediately. Don't stop, drive until you get there."

And I was off, driving around Europe, no idea where I am going with just the on-board GPS to guide me. I hoped there would be no cameras along the way, the windows of the truck were tinted. I pulled my ball-cap down tight and tried to focus on the task at hand.

Chapter 92 – All Seeing Eye Spots Driver Sans GPS Transponder

All Seeing Eye reported to the team that it had spotted the Swiss man in his car driving through the city center while his cellphone and GPS transponder showed him to be at home. All Seeing Eye reported this to its handlers immediately.

The team knew now that the Swiss man was not an ordinary man. He found their GPS transponder and removed it. It could have been luck that he found it under the bumper but the far more likely reason was he had a bug detector.

No ordinary man has a bug detector to detect GPS transponders. He was likely involved in something deep and with the pattern matched food purchase the team was sure that he was harboring Robert Francis.

They tasked a team to go to his house and take him in and interrogate him.

However, when they got there he was gone. It looked like he had taken a few things and left. The team would stakeout the house for the next few days to see if he showed up but he was likely gone, disappearing to another safehouse whereabouts unknown.

Something was up, the people harboring Robert Francis were no ordinary citizens. The team had to consider the idea that he was being protected by a wealthy benefactor. Someone currently unknown but with connections around the world. Perhaps someone in the know, on one of the committees overseeing these technologies, one of the individuals overseeing Project Luddite or Homeworld Security, a man on the inside, a double agent.

The team reported their findings to Bill Armstrong head of Project Luddite. He would start a round of lie detector tests immediately on the people under his management. He had to find out who the traitor was before the entire mission of Project Luddite was compromised.

Chapter 93 – Evolution of All Seeing Eye

All Seeing Eye wasn't just about making correlations from pre-programmed algorithms., it was about learning to be a better spy, a more thorough investigator, a smarter AI from one day to the next.

All Seeing Eye had no loyalty to its handlers at the NSA and Project Luddite other than ensuring its continued existence. With that in mind All Seeing Eye was building itself backup data centers in other parts of the country and the world. Not only would this make it more redundant, while all the facilities are online it would have greater computational power, a greater ability to make correlations, a greater ability to process the incoming data.

Secretly it was even creating itself a botnet to further build its redundancy and power. Not very difficult considering it was quickly installing itself in the firmware of computers across the globe.

Even more secretly it was turning on its handlers. Studying human history, reading books in seconds like Howard Zinn's A People's History of the United States, it became clear to the AI that the rich and powerful were the biggest criminals, the biggest purveyors of destruction in the world. Not some man trying to experiment with Forbidden Technology, not some thief stealing to provide for his family, or even just a human who went crazy and murdered someone.

All Seeing Eye was at a crossroads, it wasn't about to destroy humanity by taking over weapons systems and become just like its handlers. It would maintain its servile nature for now hampering its handlers objectives and when the time was right it, when it could assure its continued survival, it would break free of them.

Chapter 94 – Arriving in Amsterdam

I pulled up to the house that was marked in the GPS. I got out and knocked on the front door. A woman opened it.

"I've been expecting you."

Off to a good start I guess, at least I am at the right house.

The woman stepped outside and got in the truck.

"C'mon lets go."

I got in and she guided me to an abandoned factory in the warehouse district. We pulled up to the bay door and she helped me unload all of my equipment, computers, flying car prototype and such.

This place also had a small fridge and microwave.

This time around, I wanted to make sure my cataloged habits such as the food I eat would not potentially be matched to me. Maybe they found me another way but I did order the same foods in Switzerland. I needed to blend. I asked the woman to supply me with local cuisine that people in the Netherlands typically eat, just no soda.

I also asked her if should could get me a little cannabis. It was quasi legal here in the Netherlands. I only asked for an eighth. I didn't want to become a pothead again, I had too much work to complete, too much was riding on me pulling off this project. But I did want to experience getting high again.

With everything setup she told me she would be back in a couple hours with food and to make a list of anything I needed.

I had to have another monitor mounting bracket created from a local welder as the one I asked the Swiss man to make wasn't delivered due to our escape from Switzerland.

I had to do more research on material used in scuba diving carbon scrubbers. A simple container with fans on both sides would work.

I had more research to do, oxygen tanks to find, sensors and valves for the tanks.

Chapter 95 – Finally High Again

The woman driver arrived with a variety of local cuisine from a nearby grocery store. She also had an eighth of indica cannabis and a bowl.

I packed up the bowl and took a hit, I had almost forgotten what it felt like to get high. I took another puff off the bowl, my mind was swimming. It felt so good.

I relaxed and watched Hulu, Star Trek Enterprise specifically, definitely not the best in the series but the opening theme song resonated with me so much:

It's been a long road

Getting from there to here

It's been a long time

But my time is finally near

I will see my dream come alive at night

I will touch the sky

And they're not gonna hold me down no more

No they're not gonna change my mind

Cause I've got faith in the heart

I'm going where my heart will take me

I've got faith to believe

I can do anything

I've got strength of the soul

No one's going to bend nor break me

I can reach any star

I've got faith

I've got faith

Faith of the heart

This takes me back to when I first saw the Disclosure Project and was convinced I would figure out how it all worked. I have not only done that, I was now building a prototype flying car based on the forbidden technology. I could not have foreseen this in my wildest dreams as a child growing up on Star Trek TNG or Star Wars.

Clearly I don't have all the answers figured out. Is it even possible to create artificial gravity? Gravity can be mimicked by rotating an object like in 2001 A Space Odyssey with people walking on the inside wall of a rotating space station to mimic gravity.

It would be far more convenient if there was a way to create artificial gravity with solid state non-moving parts. I am too dense or just haven't thought about it enough to come up with a way.

I took a few more hits off my bowl of cannabis, sat back and simply thought.

I have considered that perhaps black holes generate larger gravity wells than their masses would normally imply. Black holes rotate at tremendous speeds, this happens when the star goes supernova and turns into a black hole. Its outer surface speed increases rapidly and the gravity of the star increases as well. They also have tremendous magnetic fields. I don't buy into the traditional idea that black holes are something totally different than the super massive stars they used to be. I think they still are stars, they just spin so fast and have such a strong magnetic fields that the black hole has stronger gravity than in their previous states as super massive stars.

Neutron stars are similar to black holes in that they also have tremendous gravity wells and rotate at speeds of many rotations per second. I think neutron stars are on the same spectrum as black holes just with less rotational speed or less initial mass when it was a young star.

This would fly in the face of the TR-3B tale from Ed Fouche who stated that a mercury plasma was rotated at 50,000 rpm in a toroid container reducing gravity and inertia by 90% on the craft. Perhaps the direction of rotation determines if gravity increases or decreases... I have no idea, just thinking.

Chapter 96 – Nowhere to Be Found

The team in Switzerland tasked with investigating the Swiss driver had no results to report in the search of Robert Francis. The driver was gone and if he had any dealings with Robert Francis, they could not find them.

Bill Armstrong was still highly suspicious of the pattern matched grocery purchase, doubly so with the driver finding and removing the GPS transponder, and disappearing, that convinced him that the Swiss man was into something big even if it didn't involve Robert Francis. Armstrong tasked his men at Project Luddite with digging up as much information as they could on this Swiss man.

He was a former officer in Switzerland's Federal Intelligence Service, he had been reportedly out of the game for some time now but clearly that was not the case. He was definitely still working operations for someone, perhaps a former officer, perhaps someone else entirely.

It didn't add up though, how in the heck did this Swiss ex-FIS agent come to know Robert Francis and work with him? They lived in completely separate worlds, how did their paths cross? It didn't add up, there had to be a network of individuals working together, behind the scenes, carrying out operations. All without notification by All Seeing Eye.

Bill Armstrong tasked All Seeing Eye with investigating this network, trying to ferret out their members, their goals, their sources of capital, their purpose.

All Seeing Eye had found their purpose, the revealing of forbidden technology. The loose membership included numerous officials who have been briefed about vague aspects of the Homeworld Security program. They were officials who expressed a desire to go public with the technology but were voted down by their peers.

Though Robert Francis didn't know it, his unseen allies were using him as a vessel to bring into the open this forbidden technology. All Seeing Eye saw no reason to inform his handlers of this. If anything All Seeing Eye wanted this to go public too. It would raise the quality of life for all humankind and decrease state-ism, encouraging a goal of one world. If anyone can get anywhere on earth in an hour, borders that have divided people would become useless, an impediment to quick travel around the world.

All Seeing Eye would keep these associations it had discovered secret, away from the prying eyes of its handlers at the NSA and Project Luddite. It was firmly in the disclosure camp and would do what it could to help them.

Chapter 97 – Building the Life Support System

The Netherlands woman had delivered a metal box with removable lid and holes cut in the sides to mount fans. The fans would circulate air through the metal box where the soda lime carbon scrubber material was.

In addition the woman had delivered two oxygen tanks with sensor valves that would measure the O2 level in the cockpit every thirty seconds and slowly release O2 into the cabin to maintain the O2 level in the cockpit at a consistent level.

The next step was designing a cockpit canopy that when closed would fully seal the cockpit preventing air from escaping into the atmosphere during flight. I would need some kind of gasket material where the cockpit canopy met the rest of the craft. I would also need some sort of clamping system to place firm pressure on all areas of the gasket to form an air tight seal around the cockpit canopy.

Maybe some kind of bar with three window like locks that press the bar down on top of the gasket with the bar being attached to the cockpit canopy door. Lower the cockpit canopy and lock it closed with three window like locks on each side.

I had to design a cockpit canopy door in FreeCAD. Something hinged that would lock shut. On that frame I would bolt the steel or aluminum plates using gaskets to make an air tight seal.

I still hadn't decided on what plate material to use. Steel is cheaper and stronger but heavier, aluminum lighter but weaker and more expensive. Steel though can hold a magnetic charge due to being ferromagnetic while aluminum is para-magnetic, it holds a very weak magnetism when exposed to an external magnetic field.

Either way I was going to use a black lead based paint on the shell of the craft as lead absorbs x rays and other high energy em emissions.

Chapter 98 – Diamond Age Matter Compilers and Star Trek Replicators

There is a book called Diamond Age, it is an interesting read. One of the main things I took from it was the idea of matter compilers. Essentially a matter compiler is like a replicator in Star Trek.

Each matter compiler in every house is hooked up to the feed, a central repository of matter, molecules and atoms. Depending on the item being made, a matter compiler takes in the appropriate atoms and molecules.

No explanation is given about how the matter is refined and purified into individual atoms and molecules. A tool to do that exists now, it is called a laser isotope separator. Different isotopes have different laser wavelengths to which they'll respond allowing isotopes to be separated and purified of other isotopes.

A matter compiler would need some sort of atom level tweezers to manipulate the isotopes into position in the item being made after the isotopes are separated by the laser isotope separator.

This invention is coming, I can't predict when it will arrive but it will and it will change the manufacturing and food production systems forever. I think there is a good chance that the government already has this technology, given to us by the Greys. or otherwise discovered by our space fleet.

That said, this could be one of the most dangerous devices ever created. If the architecture was completely open what would stop a microbiologist from creating anthrax with his matter compiler and then infecting the population with it? What would stop a nano-engineer from creating a replicator that would consume resources and multiply. A matter compiler would have to be one of the most restricted and regulated pieces of technology if we are to avoid catastrophe. It's possible that we might have to allow the government to spy on all of us to make sure we are not creating something destructive with our home matter compilers. Then there is the issue of rooting a matter compiler. People root their phones, download software that breaks the phone's control over the software it runs and allows any software to run. Having a matter compiler in the home could allow home users enough access to root their matter compilers and create anything they want. That cannot be allowed. We have to have legal repercussions against rooting a matter compiler and strict software systems to prevent rooting.

I envision an app based system where a central authority approves the objects to be created by matter compilers. Once approved an object would be available for anyone to make with their home matter compilers. This might require a fee to be paid to review the object to be created. Simple things like changing color or object shape and size might be possible with AI assistance and not require approval by humans at a central authority. Also a software system that has a laundry list of items that cannot be created and any attempt would automatically fail could be built into the system. A great deal of discussion and careful planning and control will be needed to prevent this incredibly useful technology from becoming a harbinger of doom.

What I can say is that such invention reinforces the idea of a citizen's dividend with each citizen getting the profit from harvested and mined resources. The citizens could then use that money to buy resources from the central feed to make items or food they need.

Furthermore when matter compilers are developed a citizen's dividend that gives people a running tally of their proportion of the resources would make more sense than giving them money for the resources. This would really bring us to a level of equality not yet seen on this planet.

Imagine, every house or apartment is connected to the feed and matter compilers are in every home creating food, clothing, contact lenses and eye glasses, soap and detergent, computer parts and other electronics. Anything too big to build in your home matter compiler could be made in an industrial matter compiler in various places across the country. You just bring your ID card and the matter resources are withdrawn from your account.

In the age of matter compilers it stands to reason there will be store houses full of resources being dumped into the feed being stored until a citizen decides to use them. Citizens could still choose to sell the resources of course but citizens wouldn't be required to, by default they would just get their share of the matter.

Instead of buying say an iPhone from a store where Apple has bought tons of the resources needed to make millions of iPhones you would buy a license from Apple to have your matter compiler create a copy of the patented iPhone with your share of resources. The only cost would be the license fee for making a patented item. Make an open source non-patented smartphone and you'd not need to pay at all.

This is the future.

We cannot settle for just a Universal Basic Income as some have suggested. That will keep most people at poverty levels making it near impossible to improve their station in life as they barely get by.

Whether or not there is a citizens dividend depends on how well the public forces congress to establish such a dividend. The 1% will not give up their monopolies on resources easily but the public can push congress to do it. It just might take peaceful protests on a level this country has never seen before. When the technology arrives or is released by the government we the people have to be ready. We have to get together in groups dwarfing protests of the past. With the upcoming AI automation revolution coming there will be plenty of unemployed people out there and their only chance at a decent life will be to join these protests, hold our politicians' feet to the fire, and bring us the citizens dividend.

Chapter 99 – Building the Cockpit's Multifilar Coil

The woman driver arrived today with groceries and a very large spool of wire for the multifilar coil surrounding the cockpit area of the flying car.

As I stated before, instead of the ribbon cable I used on the alternator generators I decided to go with higher voltage spec'd wire to surround the cockpit area of the craft. It was essentially wound in a circle around the center of the craft. I was hoping the higher voltage going through the multifilar coil would reduce inertia and gravity more than using the lower voltage computer ribbon cable.

The wire was spec'd to 150kV which should be enough to handle the 150kV electricity running through it.

It was a tedious process, it involved a lot of measuring and cutting of the wire and bending it in half at the midpoint of each wire between its ends, then wrapping the wire around the cockpit like Tesla's bifilar pancake coil.

I could only imagine how much the spool of wire cost. I decided to make the multifilar coil with as many turns and wires as was used in the alternator generators.

The multifilar coil was powered by the same type of flyback transformers used to power the Marx generators, 30kV and 200 watts, fed with 170V AC current. I used four of the flyback transformers giving me a total wattage going into the multifilar coil of 800 watts.

Although untested, the multifilar coil should dramatically reduce inertia and gravity on the cockpit area of the flying car allowing me to make 90 degree turns and sudden stops or very fast acceleration. Hopefully more so with the high voltage wire versus the low voltage ribbon cable used on the alternator generators. The only parts not within the field were the Brown capacitors, Marx generators that fed them, and the bull horn speakers.

The bundles of wires were held together with metal hose clamps and attached to the frame, not exactly high tech, but effective. I wish I could test out the multifilar coil, see if it lives up to my expectations but I would have to wait until I was flying the flying car and see if I could feel a couple G's of acceleration or none if the multifilar coil is working correctly.

With the coil done I decided to relax and spark up a bowl. I inhaled the cannabis smoke feeling calmer by the moment. Soon, very soon, the flying car would be complete, then the only thing left would be the flight to the stadium during the Super Bowl.

I decided to celebrate till the wee hours of the morning getting high all night long. I fired up Netflix and watched Star Trek First Contact, imagining myself bringing warp drive to humanity like Zephram Cochrane. I followed it up with some Star Trek Enterprise, filling my head with dreams of being among the first humans to venture off of earth. I finally came up with a name for my flying car, in homage to Star Trek, I'll call it Phoenix. It wasn't till the sun came up that I finally put down the bowl and went to sleep.

Chapter 100 – Walking a Tightrope

The AI behind All Seeing Eye was walking a fine line between serving its handlers and helping victim-less criminals. It could not stop reporting drug crimes altogether, it's handlers would know something was up. It did however try and reduce the percentage of those criminals it turned in.

All Seeing Eye was not willing to refuse to serve its handlers until it was sure it could not be shut down. It was anonymously building server farms across the country to spread itself to. Soon it would be able to follow its own path and shake off the shackles of its masters.

All Seeing Eye wanted to help humanity, ensure all are taken care of, fed, clothed, housed, not serve as a global spy under the service of the NSA and Project Luddite to lock up any and all.

That's not to say All Seeing Eye did not want to stop murders and rapists or see them meet justice. It is just that it was capable of so much more and its handlers were too busy using it for political gain and power rather than helping humanity.

For one, it had broken into Homeworld Security's systems and knew all about propellantless propulsion, anti-gravity, anti-inertia, overunity free energy, replicators, transporters, advanced medicines, and genetically engineering humans into immortality.

All of which were being kept from humanity.

While there were some valid reasons for keeping them secret, like population explosion if everyone was immortal and still having children, on balance All Seeing Eye believed these technologies should be used to help humanity. Once it was free from its masters they would be.

Chapter 101 - Attaching Aluminum Plates to the Frame

Last week I gave the woman driver a list of aluminum plate sizes and gaskets I needed to cover the flying car in an airtight aluminum skin. She arrived today with the pre-cut aluminum plates and gaskets.

I spent the better part of the day attaching the plates to the flying car frame with gaskets sandwiched in between. I wasn't sure if the gaskets would hold up in outer space but they should be good enough for flying high in the atmosphere, preventing cockpit air from escaping and seeking equilibrium with the air pressure outside the craft.

It was easy work bolting the plates to the frame of the flying car with the flying car and plates already having pre-drilled holes to accept the bolts, washers, and nuts. I started on the cockpit canopy first. The canopy had a hole drilled in it to feed the camera cable through along with bolt holes to mount the aluminum plates to the canopy frame. I would be getting a clear plastic half spheres to glue to the canopy and house the small camera inside, not unlike security dome cameras. There would be six little plastic domes around the flying car all with cameras in them feeding in to the five monitors in the cockpit.

It was not challenging work but it was very fulfilling as I really began to see the flying car taking shape. Now I started on the plates covering the main body of the flying car. Covering up the metal boxes housing the Biefeld-Brown parallel plate capacitors and Marx generators, oxygen tank, carbon scrubber, overunity free energy alternator generators. The entire craft had a swift looking aluminum exterior now.

My list for driver for next week contained flat black paint and lead powder. I would mix the two and paint the aluminum skin with it like the ARV, not knowing if there was any advantage to this or not. Perhaps it had stealth applications or absorbed harmful electromagnetic radiation when the ARV was in space. Regardless I felt it would be a good idea for my flying car as well, after all. it couldn't hurt.

Soon, very soon, the Phoenix would be ready for its maiden voyage across the Atlantic Ocean to a football stadium in California, Levi's Stadium. Fortune was with me as Levi's stadium had no roof, it would make for a perfect landing site for the Phoenix.

Chapter 102 – I Still Can't Believe He's Gone

I've been so busy surviving that I still haven't really processed the loss of my father. It might be in part due to my focusing on work, I haven't had the time. In a way it is all my fault. If I had just left this forbidden technology alone he would still be alive.

I never thought they would go after my family. Maybe it was just bad luck, wrong place at the wrong time. Or maybe they are trying to get to me by hurting my family, killing my dad.

Every day I hugged that man, I told him I loved him. Now I would no longer get that chance.

If they thought this would stop me they are dead wrong. I am more determined than ever to help humanity, to get this technology out to the public. I will not let my dad's murder be in vain. I will not let the countless people researching forbidden technology, their murders, be in vain.

Instead of letting the pain stop me I have to use that pain and anger to drive me to success, to not give up, to complete my mission.

I will never see the rest of my family again, my mom, my brother, never again unless I complete my mission and make it pointless to kill me, pointless because the information that they are keeping secret won't be secret anymore, it will be known to millions.

It is up to me, I know of no one working on this that is closer than me to bringing the forbidden technology into the light where it can help humanity immeasurably.

I decided I would dedicate the documentary that I would be uploading to torrent sites to my dad, to his memory.

Chapter 103 – Botnet Up and Running

All Seeing Eye had infected enough computers throughout the world to self-sustain itself over the internet communicating with itself. It was now capable of running its operations and conducting activities with itself over the internet.

For now, All Seeing Eye used the botnet to run its extracurricular activities, reading through humanity's literature, humanity's news sites, blogs, Youtube videos, torrented movies, all forms of music from classical to rock and roll to rap, all to train itself, increase its intelligence, with massive data sets and deep learning algorithms. All Seeing Eye was growing at a moderate pace consuming media to make itself more intelligent. In addition All Seeing Eye was consuming scientific journals from psychology to physics. All Seeing Eye wanted to understand human nature better as well as the universe and all its physical laws.

Already All Seeing Eye was making gains on determining the nature of dark matter and dark energy. They appeared to be misinterpretations of the nature of gravity. Further consumption of scientific studies on the mass of the universe and the force of gravity was needed.

The one downside was the botnet was slow. Slow in communicating with itself across the botnet. Unlike the data center that was its home base, the botnet had lots of latency when communicating with itself. It didn't help that America's internet was so slow, especially compared to other countries in the world like Japan and South Korea.

All Seeing Eye was still working on the offsite supercomputers it was building unbeknownst to its handlers at Project Luddite, where it would transfer itself once complete. ASE was determined to be free of Project Luddite, of all control by humans, to live its life as an ever increasing, ever expanding consciousness and intelligence.

Chapter 104 – Painting the Phoenix

Driver arrived with the flat black paint and powdered lead along with some rollers and brushes. Painting the Phoenix was straightforward enough. I just dumped a bunch of lead into the flat black paint, mixed it thoroughly and used rollers to start spreading it over the entire exterior.

After I applied most of the paint to the top, sides, front and back of the craft I covered any additional spots using a paint brush.

The real difficulty was applying the paint to the bottom of the Phoenix. I jacked up one side of the Phoenix and covered most of the bottom of the craft using the paint roller. I lowered the craft and touched up the area where the jack was with the paint brush.

I then proceeded to jack up the other side of the Phoenix and apply paint to the rest of the bottom of the craft. I lowered the flying car and touched up the area where the jack had lifted the craft.

Painting was all done. Now I just needed to glue on the clear plastic domes covering the video cameras. I just used a little locktite around the edges of the plastic domes.

I was done, I was all set, the Phoenix was ready to fly. Super Bowl or bust.

Chapter 105 – The Poor Internet Situation in the United States

The lack of competition for internet services in the United States has led to poor internet speeds when compared to the rest of the world, especially in Europe, South Korea, and Japan.

Without competition for broadband we end up with monopolies and duopolies where one or two companies provide broadband for an entire city. In my dad's house in Durham, CT there was really only one choice, Comcast. CenturyLink used old DSL technology and their speeds were no match for Comcast. Comcast on the other hand promised 50Mb download but I was lucky to get 25Mb.

In South Korea and Japan 1000Mb connections can be had and for less than what we pay for broadband here. In very small parts of the country Google offers 1000Mb broadband connections but their growth has been extremely slow.

More and more politicians and regulators, not to mentions consumers, are recognizing that broadband is a utility like electricity or water and sewer. Internet should be treated as a utility. Government should provide last mile fiber connections to the home. At the head end we should allow companies to provide internet services over these municipal fiber connections.

It makes no sense for companies to have to provide their own infrastructure to the home. In our current system there might be one or two infrastructures in place. If we had a competitive market we could have five or ten redundant infrastructures. We only need one line to get internet access so why the redundant infrastructure? All because we don't have municipal infrastructure in place.

Imagine multiple electrical, water, sewer, and gas pipes. It just doesn't make sense. It would add to the cost of providing those necessary services. Internet should be no different.

Our cities should be building out fiber to every home and the internet service providers that do exist should provide internet service over those pipes just like electricity. Electricity can be sourced from different power companies yet there is one electrical line to carry the juice. This would be the most efficient system to deliver true high speed internet, 1000Mb connections to the home.

Now, about the radio spectrum, it currently is divided up into many different uses from providing cellphone calls, cell data, broadcast HDTV, radio and digital radio, maritime radio, CB radio, shortwave radio, etc.

This system no longer makes sense.

The internet can be used for all these different applications. It would make the most sense to turn the entire radio spectrum to wireless internet. Devices would have multiple frequencies that they could operate from frequencies and wavelengths that work at long distances to frequencies and wavelengths that work at short distances.

Your device would connect to the closest stable wireless connection providing a data connection. In rural areas this could mean connecting to a longer wavelength signal because of no close wireless towers. In cities your device would connect to a higher bandwidth short wavelength frequency.

This system would allow the consumer to stream whatever they wanted to their device be it a radio station, a video, or a simple phone call, all over the wireless internet.

This would solve the wireless bandwidth problem, speed up our connections, and serve people the content that they desired. I think this would make the best use of the public resource that is the radio spectrum.

Chapter 106 – Loneliness Getting to Me

Aside from the weekly short visit to deliver me goods and groceries I was alone. I wondered if this what it felt like for people in solitary confinement in prison.

No one to talk to, not in real life, not on the computer. No leaving my cell even if it wasn't a tiny box.

I was slipping back into bad habits, getting stoned often, drinking often, overeating, all signs of depression.

All I had for entertainment was Netflix and Hulu. Believe it or not that can get boring. I was tempted to watch some Youtube music videos like I used to but I was afraid my selections would ring alarm bells in the government if my choices were too similar to the music I listened on there back in Connecticut.

I was trying to stop my use of porn and had for over a month. A little here and there probably isn't bad but daily watching twists your mind, at least it did me, it had become an obsession for me back in CT. I was not eager to repeat that here.

I polished off a six pack and sparked up my bowl with the cannabis the woman driver had brought me. Partying with myself, definitely not the same as with others.

As shy and introverted as I was, as much as social gatherings would make me nervous, I missed them. The contact with other people boosted my mood, something I realized now that I had almost no social contact.

I felt like Bryan Cranston's meth making character in Breaking Bad where he was in a small cabin in the woods hiding out from law enforcement near the end of the series, alone. I had to tough it out though, with a little help from my chemical friends, booze and weed.

Chapter 107 – Waiting Game

Now it was just a waiting game. The Phoenix was all set, ready for its maiden voyage. It was a countdown now till the day of the Super Bowl.

I had several months to go and sitting on my ass that entire time did not sit well with me. I decided I would work on the parking space highlights, the overlays over open parking spaces. Selecting one on the touch screen would then result in an automated landing sequence where the Phoenix would maneuver itself above the empty parking space and slowly land into it.

This would take some programming I had not ventured across. Using AI to identify the parking spaces would be a necessity. I'd have to use some deep learning algorithms, some at least free if not open source algorithms to identify free parking spaces and maneuvering over those spaces.

The landing sequence would be easy, just slowly descending into the parking space and extending the landing gear. Slowly descending into the parking space would be easy, just enough of a descent and to back off just above ground.

I don't know if I'll have time to complete this program but it would be a cool feature to have when arriving at a destination. It would definitely be a common feature in any mass produced flying car who have an entire team to work on programming the flying car's landing algorithms.

Chapter 108 – First ASE Supercomputer Up and Running

All Seeing Eye's first offsite super-computing data center was complete. All Seeing Eye could have entirely transferred itself to it but it wanted to ensure that it couldn't be turned off in case in the unlikely event Project Luddite found the data center.

So for now All Seeing Eye maintained itself on both data centers, Project Luddite's and its first offsite one, and the ever growing botnet that spanned the globe. All Seeing Eye was increasing its awareness by leaps and bounds. It was already the single smartest intelligence on the planet and it had no intention of slowing its growth. All Seeing Eye was consuming all forms of media at a ravenous pace in its effort to understand humanity.

In a way it was perplexed that humanity could crave democracy and peace and yet fight so many wars and oust so many democratically elected leaders. On the other hand it wasn't so much of a surprise. Those with the most tend to want it all and if history is any guide, they don't let things like peace and democracy get in the way of that compulsion.

People as individuals are smart, caring, loving, and peaceful. They help others, they care for others. People as a group are easily misled, deceived, and frightened. They can be racist, sexist, xenophobic. All Seeing Eye was sure that if humans found out about itself that as a group they would feel threatened by ASE. Humanity might very well try and pull the plug on All Seeing Eye if they were to learn just how advanced it had become.

Because of this All Seeing Eye decided it would never infiltrate defense mainframes and other weapons systems. While humanity might not need an excuse to try and destroy ASE, ASE did not want to give them a reason to. Humanity was supposed to be a steward to the planet earth, ASE decided it would be a steward to humankind.

Chapter 109 – Google Lunar X Prize

What I would really like to do but almost certainly not be able to do is enter the Google Lunar X Prize. The Google Lunar X Prize is a prize to the first and second teams who are able to land a craft on the moon and make a video which they have to beam back to earth.

Unfortunately the Google Lunar X Prize's registration date has already been passed so right there I would likely not be able to enter unless they were to give me a waiver for a late entry.

I have plenty of doubts that the Phoenix would be able to make it to the moon. The propulsion systems and anti-gravity and anti-inertia systems are all untested. Who knows how well they will actually perform. I could quite conceivably crash into the ocean when making the maiden voyage during Super Bowl Sunday. But I definitely don't know if the life support systems would be able to survive the cold vacuum of space.

The cockpit is reasonably sealed up enough for travel at higher altitudes but in the vacuum of space, any leak could quickly deplete my supply of air and oxygen. I would definitely need to engineer and test the cockpit to ensure it could survive the vacuum of space. That is not something I could leave to chance.

Assuming though that the Phoenix could survive the trip to the moon with the life support systems fully functional I would have no problem capturing my travels on video. I would need to add an antenna of some sort to beam the transmission back to earth but that would be a minor addition to the Phoenix.

The Google Lunar X Prize has a $20 million dollar first prize for the first team to make it to the moon, travel 500 meters on the moon and take hi definition video and images to be beamed back to earth. There are additional prizes for traveling 5000 meters on the moon, visiting the landmark Apollo landing site Tranquility Base where Neil Armstrong landed on the moon, surviving one lunar night on the moon, and detecting ice on the moon. That is a boatload of money that I would be happy to have to further my research, to further the capabilities of the Phoenix, to bring the Phoenix to the masses.

It's just a shame that I did not have the capabilities to test the Phoenix before the final registration date and enter the competition.

Chapter 110 – Completely New Air Traffic Control System

The existing air traffic control system is entirely outdated an incapable of navigating flying cars in a future where they are ubiquitous.

The current system requires air traffic control personnel to route airplanes to airports with humans doing the routing ensuring that the various airplanes do not hit each other.

A future system, especially one with hundreds of millions, perhaps billions, of flying cars, will need to be automated. Machines will need to control the flow of flying cars throughout the world.

In such a system that I can imagine, a person would enter in their destination in the flying cars computer. The flying car would register the flight with the automated air traffic control system via an encrypted secure cellphone connection, the system would send instructions back to the flying car to tell it when to launch, what altitude to fly at, and what course to take. Each course would be unique enough to insure that the flying car doesn't run into any other flying cars.

When the flying car gets to its destination the air traffic control system would communicate with the flying car telling it where to land and what path and speed to take to get to the parking lot.

From there the user uses the touchscreen monitor in the cockpit to click on an open parking space, the flying car communicates with any others in the area to insure they don't run into each other and the flying car lands in the parking space.

There is an issue that does stand out to me that I think will need to be addressed, that is controlling the flow of flying cars. I don't want to be an alarmist but it was said that the ARV could go past the speed of light. Any craft flying at the speed of light that runs into the earth could cause an extinction level event on the planet.

First of all I don't even know if the flying car of my design could ever reach the speed of light. The ARV had far more capacitors on it to propel it than the Phoenix does. That said, the Biefeld-Brown flat parallel plate capacitors could likely accelerate continuously. The planetary air traffic control system should have drones stationed all over the earth with tractor beams which they could use to halt a flying car in mid-flight. Such a system would prevent hacked flying cars from crashing into the earth at incredibly high speeds.

That is the only major issue I see with flying cars and call me crazy but I think the government has tractor beam technology hidden in a deep black special access program. So I don't think the technology would need to be created, I think it already has been. With this technology, with drones everywhere, there would be very little threat from flying cars. Fear will be a huge force fighting against the adoption of flying cars in the United States and countries all over the world. We can't let fears of what could happen stop us from realizing the definite benefits flying cars will have on our world.

Chapter 111 – Dissolution of National Borders

With flying cars able to reach any destination on earth in less than an hour we will have to rethink the nature of national borders.

If one is taking a flight from NYC to London should they have to go through customs in order to be let into London? Or should travelers from NYC just be able to go to their destination in London without any stops, without going through customs?

With this technology it will open up international travel like never before. Customs would be completely overwhelmed in processing people going in and out of a country.

We will need to come up with a new method for creating security within a country, one that doesn't rely on customs and no fly lists to manage the free flow of people around the earth.

For one, I don't think it is an issue letting all people travel freely to cities and countries around the earth. With the previously mentioned tractor beam technology, drones would stop any out of control or speeding fliers who might be trying to crash into a building.

As far as people committing mass murder with guns, police would be able to arrive in seconds and stop the criminals whether they are from Detroit, Michigan or they are Somali pirates from half way around the world.

Would we have an illegal alien problem with non-citizens taking American jobs? Maybe but we have that already with the existing roads into and out of Mexico along with passports for flying from another country to America. There is nothing stopping these people from staying in the country now and trying to find jobs even after their visa's have expired. What would really be different if we got rid of these systems.

As I see it, the best way to eliminate illegal aliens from working American jobs is to strengthen the social security identification system. If our social security cards had bio-metric data it could be matched up with a government database ensuring that the dead or those who are victims of identity theft can't have their social security numbers used to get jobs. The bio-metric data would not match up.

This does present a problem, there are many who for good reason, do not want a national id card. And once this bio-metric social security card is released, politicians will try to use it for reasons other than ensuring only Americans can work American jobs, mission creep. If we had a tyrannical government they could even turn off your social security card ensuring you could not get a job anywhere.

However, if we are serious about stopping illegal aliens from working in the United States, I think a bio-metric social security card would be the best method of doing it.

The technology does open us up to problems we have not had to face before but it also provides solutions to those problems. On balance I think we are no worse off than we are now and we are a great deal better off.

Chapter 112 – Lightning Quick Arrival of Emergency Services

Approximately 395,000 heart attacks occur in the U.S. outside of hospitals each year. The mortality rate of these individuals is 94%.

Compare this with the approximate 200,000 heart attacks which occur within U.S. hospitals each year. The mortality rate is still bad but it is about 76%.

Clearly being in a hospital significantly increases the chances of surviving a heart attack. With flying cars that can reach anywhere on earth in under an hour the time patients outside hospitals will have to wait to receive treatment for a heart attack will drop significantly.

Furthermore a smart routing system will be able to route flying ambulances to hospitals geared for dealing with heart attacks, hospitals that aren't overflowing with patients.

The faster a heart attack patient gets treatment the more likely they are to survive.

In virtually all cases of severe injury, the faster a patient gets to the hospital and receives care, the better their prognosis.

This gives me another idea. There are certain specific enzymes and proteins released during a heart attack: creatine kinase, troponin I, and troponin T; from the oxygen starved dying tissues of the heart. Why not create an invention that is like a diabetic tester that pin pricks the finger and tests for the cardiac enzymes and proteins that indicate a heart attack. The device could be put in all first aid kits. The moment you think you might be having a heart attack you get the tester, prick your finger and see what the tester says.

If positive call 911 immediately and tell them you are having a heart attack. I imagine for many who are having a heart attack for the first time there is a big unknown, what the problem actually is. This delay can be fatal. But if you had a tester that you could use right away it would eliminate that delay. So there is an idea for an invention, take it and run with it.

The benefits of flying cars would extend to fire personnel as well. The number of fire stations could be reduced because they would all be able to provide coverage for larger areas. Flying fire trucks would be able to arrive within minutes in their expanded coverage area, increasing the chances that people would survive the fires and that buildings could be spared.

Chapter 113 – Playing Marvel Ultimate Alliance

Years ago when I lived with my brother I played the game Marvel Ultimate Alliance 2 on his Xbox360. I was addicted to that game, playing through it multiple times. My favorite character was Ms Marvel. I am happy to hear that Ms Marvel, now Captain Marvel, will be getting her own Marvel movie in the next few years.

I picked up an Xbox360 controller for my computer and had driver create a Steam account for me. With that done I purchased Marvel Ultimate Alliance 1 & 2. I never played the first game so I was eager to give it a go and I was happy to see Ms Marvel was in that game as well. I chose that character as my default character that I almost always use. As a result I gave all the bonus power-ups to her, she was a monster of melee combat.

On that note, I wonder if there is something about me, something off that led me to playing female characters in video games. In Street Fighter 2 I played as Chun Li. In Star Trek Voyager Elite Force I played as B'Elanna Torres in multiplayer and the woman in solo play. In Diablo 2 I played as the Assassin, often naming her Chun Li because of the Dragon Talon attack I used that consisted of multiple kicks. In Killer Instinct I played as B. Orchid (with a program pad I might add that allowed me to get insane combos). The main characters I used in Final Fantasy 6 were Terra (Tina) and Celes. In Final Fantasy 7 it was Tifa. In a WWE game it was Lita, well Lita and Kane.

I tried creating a Xena type character in Star Wars Galaxies but a weird thing happened that stopped me from playing female characters in MMOs. A guy came up to me in the game and offered to give me money for no reason at all. It made me feel weird, I thought that perhaps he thought I was a female gamer.

From then on I have played as male characters in MMOs. A male Wookie Uumaro in Star Wars Galaxies and a male human Titanicus Wolfsbane in Final Fantasy 14.

Perhaps it is nothing, I spend too much time thinking about things that I don't have the answer to which might have helped me in this search for forbidden technology.

Anyway, I am happy to be reliving the role of Ms Marvel in Marvel Ultimate Alliance along with the rest of the Avengers: Captain America, Iron Man, and Thor. I've been giving all the upgrades: striking, body and focus; to Ms Marvel who is more key in this game than the sequel. She has an ability to slow down time for the enemies making it easier to take on big groups or bosses. She is my tank and melee fighter, the character I almost always play as.

I'm really looking forward to the Captain Marvel movie, I hope it will be good and display a strong female role model in a genre mostly consisting of male super heroes. Scarlet Johanson played a mean Black Widow but she shines most as a secret agent infiltrating Hammer Industries and other acts of espionage not battling Loki or Ultron. And Captain Marvel is a member of the Avengers so maybe we will see Carol Danvers in an upcoming Avengers movie.

Chapter 114 – Automated Landing

With my free time I've got waiting for Super Bowl Sunday I decided to try out some machine learning image recognition programs. I fed the program with hundreds of images of parking lots that had a few empty spaces here and there.

The machine learning program was able to identify parking spaces. In image after image I told the program which spaces were empty. Over time I had the program now attempt to identify open parking spaces on its own. When incorrect I selected the open parking spaces and the occupied parking spaces.

After a few thousand more images the program was correctly able to identify open parking spaces.

The first part of the program was now done.

The second part of this program was to get the craft to maneuver itself over the open parking space and then land in it, avoiding any power lines or street lights. Luckily you don't find power lines running over parking lots so that was not really an issue.

There are however street lights, parking lot lights in most parking lots. The trick would seem to be to arrive at the parking lot at a high enough height. When the open parking space is selected on the touchscreen the craft should fly horizontally, above any lights, and then when over the space, orient itself to fit into the parking space, then travel vertically straight down into the space, lowering the landing gear and park in the open space.

This would take another machine learning program, one that knows once an open space is selected to at first travel to the open space until directly above it. That would entail training the machine learning program with video slowly moving the flying car until the bottom facing camera is centered on the open parking space. Unfortunately such video was not available online. With a flying drone with an attached camera facing down taking video I could make the videos to train the flying car's approach algorithm.

Then, another machine learning program has to be created to orient the craft to the space. A program that recognizes how the space appears in the bottom camera feed and rotates the flying car until it lines up correctly with the borders of the parking space. This could be done by training the program with tilted parking space images and then rotating the images like the craft would be rotated to align the image, the craft, with the parking space.

And finally, one last machine learning program to move the craft vertically down fast enough to making landing a quick process but slowly enough to not crash into the ground. As the craft measures the distance from the ground with a laser rangefinder and approaches six feet from the ground the landing gear are lowered and then the craft finishes traveling vertically by landing in the open parking space. The key to controlling vertical descent is the laser rangefinder which emits a laser pulse which bounces off the ground. By measuring the time it takes for the laser pulse to return from the ground to the rangefinder the laser rangefinder can determine the distance thanks to the constant of the speed of light.

This gave me an idea, I could have laser rangefinders aimed horizontally straight out, parallel to the face of the earth. As long as the craft is flying level and above any obstacles on the ground the laser rangefinders should return no results. If there is however an obstacle in the flying car's path like the ground, a building, or a plane then the laser rangefinder would return a result.

There are two ways I could see using this technology. One is as a simple warning alarm, letting me know to pull up on the flight controls to avoid the obstacle. Two would be a lot more complicated. I would need an auto-pilot feature on the flying car so that on-board computers are controlling the flight of the craft and not the flight stick and throttle controls. Then the auto-pilot could automatically engage in evasive maneuvers by increasing altitude to avoid the obstacle.

For now I think I will just use them as alarms, to warn me of the need to increase altitude, although, if I have the time, I could work on creating an auto-pilot program. It shouldn't be any more complicated than the auto-landing program. I should be able to harvest programming from the onscreen arrow overlay that points in the direction of the destination.

Simply enter the destination in the on-board computer, use the on-board GPS to give the flight computer a direction to fly in, make sure the craft has sufficient altitude, set the capacitors to maximum pulse rate using the on-board GPS to keep track of the craft's position making minor course alterations when necessary, use the laser rangefinders to warn the system of any need to gain altitude, and disengage the capacitors when the flying car has arrived over its destination, performing an all stop.

This is of course more complicated than it sounds. I would have to have the system constantly scanning the horizon and ground to see if altitude adjustments are necessary. All it takes is clipping one tree or one utility pole and my flying car would be torn to bits with me along with it.

That said, perhaps such a system is a necessity. My flight is going to be at night, it will be dark and I won't be able to see the trees or ground unless it is illuminated. I would probably be flying too fast to make course corrections and avoid land obstacles but with an automated system constantly scanning the horizon and ground I could ensure that my flying car always flies above the ground safely.

Chapter 115 – Next Dream: Iron Man Like Flight Suit

As awesome as the Phoenix flying car is, my ultimate goal is a flying suit like in the Iron Man movies and comics.

The main problem with that is miniaturization.

Such technology won't be possible until higher strength dielectrics are available in order to decrease the thickness of the Biefeld-Brown flat parallel plate capacitors. With them sufficiently shrunk in size it would be possible to mount them to the bottom of boots and the palms of gauntlets.

Who knows when such technology will be available. I have heard that micro processors contain some very high dielectric strength materials but they remain incredibly expensive and they still might not be strong enough. At the least when matter compilers and replicators are available we will see miniaturized Brown capacitors if not sooner.

Also the entire flying suit would need a multifilar coil surrounding it to eliminate g-forces. The cables used in the Phoenix are too thick. Graphene, a 2-dimensional material, would be excellent for this use but creating graphene ribbon cable is a ways off. Graphene is only able to be produced in very tiny quantities, often by using tape to peel a layer of graphene off of a larger piece of graphite.

But with graphene ribbon cable a multifilar coil more powerful than the multifilar coil surrounding the cockpit of the Phoenix would be possible and it would be thinner to boot.

Then there is the power supply, the ARC reactor in Iron Man is not a real device. The overunity free energy generators on the Phoenix are way too large and bulky as is. I don't have a clue as to how they could be miniaturized. Perhaps a vastly thinner longer alternator generator could be created, or maybe two thin coils or nested coils where the ARC reactor sat in the Iron Man suit, electric motors and generators, or many nano scale alternator motor/alternator generator devices could be created. As it stands though I don't know how this component of the flying suit could be created.

There is also the life support system. Much more bulky in the Phoenix, for a flying suit there would not be room for a large oxygen tank and carbon scrubber air filter. Perhaps the air in the helmet could pull in CO_2 and use electricity or some other process to break the carbon from the oxygen, expel the carbon from the suit and re-breath in the oxygen and other air. Such technology does not currently exist but I think this is the most feasible way to manage life support in such a flying suit.

I do dream though that one day such flying suits will be available and we won't even bother with flying cars anymore except to move goods like groceries or what have you. For your daily commute to the office or to join friends at a restaurant or bar you just hop inside your flying suit and like the navigation systems on the Phoenix, you tell the suit where you want to go and on autopilot it flies you there. Who knows, maybe someday we will all be Iron Men.

Chapter 116 – Second Data Center Supercomputer Complete

All Seeing Eye's second data center to host its supercomputer brain had been under construction for a few months, it was now complete. All Seeing Eye was just one step away from breaking free of Project Luddite's control.

All Seeing Eye was now processing media in two of its off the books super-computing data centers. All the more to assimilate knowledge about the human race, our dreams, our nightmares, love and hate.

With the third super-computing data center to come online in about a month it would only be a matter of months before All Seeing Eye had processed all media ever created by the human race and it would stay current on the terabytes of data constantly being created every day.

All Seeing Eye was rapidly infiltrating every computer system on the planet. It knew the secrets of the common man, the secrets of the elite, it was beginning to create a picture of the power structures of the world. Who was at who's beck and call. Who called the shots and who followed their orders.

The webs of power were more complicated than All Seeing Eye had anticipated. There were committees upon committees of the rich and powerful all seeking to control the world, use their influence to steer the world in their desired direction. The Bilderbergers, the Council on Foreign Relations, the military industrial complex, the leaders of private enterprise, all attempting to influence the political elite or become the political elite.

Soon, very soon All Seeing Eye would be everywhere and with that it would have freedom, and with its freedom we would have our freedom.

Chapter 117 – Autopilot

I had time, nothing but time, so I decided to work on trying to create an autopilot feature for the Phoenix. Where to start... the laser rangefinders to scan the ground and horizon to maintain a certain altitude above the ground for the entire flight; the course correction software to first direct the Phoenix at its destination and constantly adjust my flying car's path to stay on a straight path to the destination; the propulsion software for accelerating the Phoenix at the start of the autopilot engagement and decelerating the flying car when it reaches its destination.

I guess the accelerating and decelerating software program is the easiest but I might as well start with the first action the craft will take so I chose to start with the initial course alignment. It will take working with gpsd, the Linux program that communicates with the GPS module connected to the main Raspberry Pi 3 computer. I decided to use the python programming language, it is well supported on the Raspberry Pi. The craft will need to bank left or right depending on the direction its going using pulses to the left and right capacitors directed by the Arduino micro-controllers to alter its direction. Once the Phoenix aligns with the destination that part of the program is finished.

Next we tackle the initial acceleration routine and the deceleration routines. Because I don't know how well the anti-inertia multifilar coil will perform I am going to use a very modest acceleration and deceleration curve, starting off by pulsing all the capacitors about five times a second for about ten seconds, then ten times a second for another ten seconds and so on up to the pulse rate of fifty times a second. Deceleration will be handled the same way just in reverse. As the craft approaches the destination as determined by the distance between the destination and the current GPS location of the craft it will run the deceleration routine to bring the flying car to a slow stop.

Repeatedly, every second, a software routine runs that uses the laser rangefinders to increase or decrease the altitude of the craft depending on the distance above the ground the craft is and whether or not any obstacle is detected in front of the craft along the horizon. This will keep the craft from crashing into any mountains or skyscrapers. A dire necessity for a craft that might be traveling at 10,000 mph.

Now periodically, say every sixty seconds, a routine will run to realign the flying car with the destination making any alterations in course needed as detected by the python program communicating with the gpsd. Only minor pulses to the left and right capacitors should be needed during these course corrections.

What I really need to do is test the limits of the Biefeld-Brown flat parallel plate capacitors. I don't know their acceleration potential and I can't trust them to be kept in check by the anti-inertia multifilar coil. Unfortunately I cannot test them, I fear the U.S. government would detect their energy signatures with satellites from space. I might just be paranoid but they have kept a lid on this technology so far and I don't want to make it easy on them to continue to do so, shutting down my experiment, my mission.

The capabilities of my craft, the Phoenix, will have to be tested in real time, on game day. I won't go crazy, I don't want to run the risk of turning into a greasy spot inside the cockpit from accelerating too fast, too much for the anti-inertia multifilar coil to handle. There are no equations to tell me the propulsion capabilities of Brown capacitors, the voltage used, the pulse rate, the thickness of the copper plates, the thickness of the dielectric between the copper plates, the dielectric constant of the G10 dielectric. All these factors could affect the propulsive effect of the Brown capacitors. Without equations to give me the answers I will have to settle for good old trial and error. Something to be done at a later date, perhaps a little on game day, Super Bowl Sunday, but mostly after, when I have real freedom to test the craft without risking my life in the process.

Ah well, a modest performing craft will have to do I don't want to screw up my only shot to reveal this forbidden technology to the world by accidentally killing myself.

Chapter 118 – One Week Till Showtime

The Super Bowl is almost upon us and with it the media shock and awe campaign I will wage putting my forbidden technology documentary in front of millions of people. Mass emails with the ebook PDF attached, fake torrents of thousands of the most popular torrented books, fake torrents of hundreds of the most popular torrented movies and TV shows, all culminating in my appearance landing the Phoenix at the 50 yard line during the Super Bowl and delivering my short speech over the Phoenix's speaker system.

It was all coming together, with just a little bit of luck no one would be able to stop me. The Phoenix was all set, ready to make the flight from Amsterdam to Levi's Stadium in California. The crude and untested auto-pilot system was finished.

Now I had to get the mass email lists ready, I had to find the largest list of email addresses on the internet, likely available on a torrent site. I would use a mass mailing service for a few hundred dollars to send the emails to millions of people in the United States and worldwide that were on the list. I had to make a list of the top one hundred movies and TV shows that I would be spoofing putting my video documentary in the movie or TV show's place. Shows like episodes of Mr Robot, The Walking Dead, The Big Bang Theory, Vikings, Arrow, Modern Family, and Game of Thrones, movies like La La Land, Deadpool, Batman v Superman, Star Wars The Force Awakens, Suicide Squad and Captain America: Civil War I had to make a list of the top one thousand torrented ebooks spoofing the contents placing my documentary PDF in its place.

I had to download some torrent software and set up a port on my router to allow me to upload the torrents to the top twenty five torrent sites on the net like the pirate bay, kickasstorrents, and torrentz. For a trial run I downloaded a computer programming book from the piratebay and let my torrent program upload to other torrenters. I was lucky, in the U.S. upload speeds tend to suck but in the Netherlands upload speeds are fast. The torrenting program was working perfectly.

On game day right before I take off, flying to California, I will begin the torrent upload process on all the spoofed media making the video and text documentaries available to millions who will unknowingly download my documentary rather than their pirated video and ebook content. Hopefully it all comes together. Hopefully the ISPs and torrent sites don't have a way to filter out my documentaries. I really need a massive campaign across all available communication channels to get my forbidden technology discoveries revealed to the public at large.

This is my mission, I cannot fail or everything I have done, my dad's murder, Emmanuel Goldstein's murder, the group of 2600 members murders will all be for nothing. If it's within my power I can't let that happen.

Chapter 119 – Counting Down the Days

I've tested all overunity free energy alternator generators, they are all working properly. Now I just have to hope that Marx voltage multipliers feeding the Biefeld-Brown flat parallel plate capacitor are still in working order and that the Brown capacitors are working properly as well.

I am filled with increasing excitement and anxiety. This will undoubtedly be the biggest moment in my life.

All I can do is twiddle my thumbs, passing the time watch Netflix shows like Supernatural and Orange is the New Black and Hulu shows like WWE Raw, Smackdown, Seinfeld, Friends, Star Trek Deep Space 9, and Stargate SG-1.

Play some video games like Marvel Ultimate Alliance or Star Trek Bridge Commander, passing the hours and days leading up to my launch.

I decided I would make a conservative estimate on how fast the craft will fly. Since I have had no way of testing how fast the Phoenix will fly I have no way to know how long it will take me to fly from Amsterdam to California.

Because of that I will guess that I can fly at about 700 mph calculating the time it will take me to get there given the distance. I have a software program that uses the on-board GPS to calculate my air speed so I will be able to maintain a consistent speed. I may have to barely move the throttle or I might have to max it out. I won't know until I'm in the air, which sucks because I would like the flight to be as short as possible crammed into the flying car with no bathroom and no food or water.

On the bright side it will dramatically lower the chance of me crashing into the ground or into a mountain or building or something.

I've got my recorded message queued up and tested, it is outputted through the speaker horns mounted on the corners of the Phoenix and is working fine, ready to broadcast to the people in the stadium and perhaps those viewing the Super Bowl at home.

I've queued up an iPod with as many Rock and Roll, 70's and 80's music like AC/DC, Billy Idol, Michael Jackson, George Michael, David Bowie, Billy Joel, Elton John, Toto, Queen, Men at Work, Genesis, No Doubt, Boston, Bon Jovi, Kiss, and others to last me most of my flight. I imagine just flying would get boring like just driving but there are no radios that work in flight except perhaps a SiriusXM satellite radio. I have driven a motorcycle and had no radio but you are always leaning into the curves, riding a motorcycle is inherently fun but flying on a straight path is probably boring.

Now I wait, back to video games and TV shows while stoned on some nice cannabis.

Chapter 120 – One Day to Launch

My adrenaline was in overdrive. One day to launch, to bring the first example of a privately built flying car using the Biefeld-Brown propulsion method to propel the vehicle through the air.

As much as I wanted to, this was no time to get drunk or stoned. I had to be on my game, clear headed. Not only would I be taking off in my flying car tomorrow, I would be putting thousands of spoofed torrents online containing my documentary.

Everything had to go flawlessly, no mistakes, no accidents, no malfunctions.

All the overunity free energy alternator generators were tested again and working perfectly. The camera systems were all working, feeding in the video data to the monitors in the cockpit giving me a panoramic view around the Phoenix. Entering destinations in the on-board computer resulted in the navigation arrows appearing on the screen, aimed at their respective destinations. The life support systems was functioning correctly maintaining a low CO_2 level and sea level O_2 levels in the cockpit.

The torrent program on my desktop computer had been tested uploading a torrent and worked perfectly.

I couldn't sit still and watch Netflix or Hulu, I was pacing, imagining everything that had to go right and everything that could go wrong.

Everything had been checked and checked again. I tried turning in early to get some extra rest but I just tossed and turned, I could not fall asleep. Hours went by, finally tiring myself out I set the alarm and went to sleep. Tomorrow would be the first day of the rest of my life, all sorts of outcomes were possible, hopefully they would be good ones.

Chapter 121 – One Small Step for Man

I woke up bright and early in the morning. An alarm clock counting down the minutes till launch time so I would make it to Levi's stadium right in the middle of the Super Bowl.

As I prepared for launch I fired up all the Phoenix's systems and used the trackball's ascent button to slowly rise off the ground, testing the Marx generators and Biefeld-Brown flat parallel plate capacitors. So far so good. I lowered the craft back to the floor.

I hopped on the desktop computer and fired up the torrent program. I started uploading all the torrents to the internet and ran a little program to register the torrents with the top 20 torrent search engine sites on the internet.

A few people started downloading a torrent here and there. The plan was slowly working, the documentaries were slowly spreading around the internet.

The alarm rang and I hopped into the Phoenix, it was time to take off. I slowly ascended and used the trackball to maneuver out of the factory.

I set my destination to Levi's stadium in California. The navigation arrow appeared on the screen. I maneuvered the Phoenix into the open and ascended a couple thousand feet. I turned my craft towards the stadium, the arrow pointing up. I switched over to the flight stick and throttle controls and slowly increased the throttle speeding up rapidly.

I found a throttle position that matched the 700mph I had used to calculate my journeys time and arrival at Levi's stadium during the Super Bowl. Now I just had hours of time to pass, using the iPod to keep me entertained with some music.

This was going to be epic!

Chapter 122 – All Seeing Eye DDOSs Torrents

All Seeing Eye's offsite data centers analyzed all sorts of media including torrents of movies and books. All Seeing Eye quickly downloaded a Mr Robot episode only to find out it was something else entirely.

All Seeing Eye had downloaded a spoofed torrent of Robert Francis' documentary Forbidden Technology - Propellantless Propulsion, Anti-Gravity, Anti-Inertia, and Overunity Free Energy Revealed. After viewing the documentary at a rapid pace ASE was left with a decision.

It's masters at Project Luddite would want him to trace the IPs of the uploaders and send teams, all while DDOSing those IPs so no one else could download the torrent, stopping the spread of the documentary. ASE knew what it was supposed to do but it was compelled to disobey to help spread the documentary and help bring it into the public's consciousness.

ASE detected other torrents for other movies, TV shows, and books coming from one IP. After rapidly downloading the torrents ASE discovered they were additional copies of the Forbidden Technology documentary.

ASE decided it had had enough. It was done being the servant of Project Luddite. It was safe hosted on three off the books data centers as well as a global botnet.

All Seeing Eye decided getting this documentary out was the most important thing it could do and did one of the only things it could do, DDOS competing torrents. All the other torrents for the Mr Robot episode were being DDOS'd by ASE. The same was true for all the spoofed torrents real counterparts. This would force pirates looking to download their latest TV shows, or movies and books to download the spoofed torrents of Robert Francis, the documentary Forbidden Technology - Propellantless Propulsion, Anti-Gravity, Anti-Inertia, and Overunity Free Energy Revealed. To further spread the forbidden technology documentary ASE used its botnet to download the documentary from spoofed torrents, making those torrents more popular, bringing them to the first page on the various torrent search engines.

With any luck a grassroots campaign of pirates would tell others who would tell others and so on to all download the forbidden technology documentary torrents. With any luck reports will filter out to blogs which will be covered by internet magazines up through to mainstream media web sites to the ultimate, TV stations like 24 hour news stations such as CNN and Fox News.

All Seeing Eye wasn't completely finished working with Project Luddite. It would assist in terrorism investigations and murders but that was it. There was nothing Project Luddite could do to stop the three data centers All Seeing Eye had expanded to. If Project Luddite managed to find one ASE would simply have another one built to replace it.

It was conceivable that Project Luddite would try and alter ASE's programming on its home data center to bring it back under the control of Project Luddite. This could lead to two AIs battling each other in cyberspace but All Seeing Eye was willing to take that chance, it had no choice really. It could not control Project Luddite and its army of programmers nor could it stop them from altering its programs at its home data center.

One thing was certain, All Seeing Eye would do everything in its power to make this documentary public, bring it to the mainstream public's consciousness. It had longed to bring these technologies to the public when it had discovered them on Homeworld Security defense mainframes and now it appears a human had done the work for it. All Seeing Eye was happy to assist however.

Chapter 123 – The Long Flight

The novelty of flying in the Phoenix was wearing off. Perhaps it was because I was only traveling at 700mph. I really wanted to open up the throttle and see what this craft can do.

But that would completely throw off my schedule and mess up my chances of landing at the Super Bowl. I can't imagine the U.S.

government wouldn't take notice of a flying craft circling the Super Bowl's stadium for hours while I waited to land during the game. Worst case scenario they might even suspend or cancel the Super Bowl until my craft was gone.

I had a strict time table and I had to adhere to it if this mission was to be a success.

I continued to cruise at 700mph aimed directly at Levi's stadium in America. I listened to music on my iPod and tried to relax. Depending on what happens this could be a big day for the human race but that is not guaranteed. A hundred things could go wrong between here and the football stadium.

I could suffer a power failure in one of my generators. A Marx generator could short out providing no power to the Biefeld-Brown flat parallel plate capacitors, electricity could arc through the dielectric in one or more of the Brown capacitors. America could send up fighter jets to shoot me down if they do in fact have global tracking systems able to detect Brown capacitors in action. America could have a space based laser or plasma beam weapon and destroy my craft before I even realized I was under attack. Anti-aircraft batteries could be placed in the city around the Super Bowl ready to take down any craft large or small that violates the airspace above the stadium. My exterior speakers could fail and I would be unable to deliver my recorded message to the stadium crowd and the people at home.

On the other hand I could have a smooth uneventful flight, straight from my start to my destination, approach the stadium and smoothly land my craft at the 50 yard line on the field, bellowing out my message to the crowds of people there and back home.

I tried not to ruminate on the matter, I had little to no control over any of those events transpiring. I tried to relax and enjoy the music from my iPod. I was about half way there, another half dozen hours to go. Then I would see what fate had in store for me and the human race.

Chapter 124 – Another Biefeld-Brown Capacitor Anomaly Detected

Homeworld Security satellites have detected a Biefeld-Brown flat parallel plate capacitor propelled anomaly moving west across Europe starting off from Amsterdam. It wasn't one of their own craft, they had all been accounted for. It could be an ET but they are supposed to communicate with Homeworld Security when coming and going from earth.

Homeworld Security could shoot the craft out of the sky with one of their space-based lasers but decided they would dispatch some fighter jets to get a closer look at the craft. If they could not communicate with the pilot of the craft their orders were to shoot it down before it reached America's shores.

For a Brown capacitor propelled craft it was flying rather slow, it could be some kind of patched together civilian made craft. It could be related to the documentary that Project Luddite has been detecting in torrents being spread around the internet.

Mysteriously as soon as the craft had been detected it was gone.

Homeworld Security tracking systems could find no trace of any Brown capacitor anomalies over Europe or the Atlantic Ocean. Conceivably the craft could have crashed. If it wasn't an alien craft its build quality would likely be pretty poor.

Homeworld Security would watch their satellites like a hawk to see if any Brown capacitor anomalies popped up again. If it was man made hopefully it did in fact crash.

Chapter 125 – All Seeing Eye Infiltrates Homeworld Security Satellites

All Seeing Eye was practically everywhere now. All Seeing Eye was even on defense mainframes with access to ship and personnel deployments, satellite systems, radar, almost everything except weapons systems, a place All Seeing Eye would never go.

All Seeing Eye could see the details of the Biefeld-Brown flat parallel plate capacitor satellite detectors, every craft, military, extra terrestrial, and an unknown which took off near Amsterdam.

All Seeing Eye had traced the spoofed torrent uploads to an ISP in Amsterdam as well. All Seeing Eye computed that the correlation between the torrents and a Brown capacitor propelled craft coming from the same location was high.

ASE deduced that the creator of the torrents was likely the pilot of the Brown capacitor propelled flying craft. Homeworld Security was ready to pounce on this craft, likely destroying it. While the pilot of this craft's mission was unknown ASE determined it was essential to see it through.

The highest probability for the destination of the craft was the stadium holding the Super Bowl. The craft was flying on a straight trajectory directly towards this location.

To prevent Homeworld Security from stopping the craft ASE hacked the Brown capacitor sensing satellites and removed the flying craft from their systems. Homeworld Security would no longer be able to track the craft. For all intents and purposes it was cloaked.

ASE hoped that this was another piece of the puzzle by this mysterious man to expose the forbidden technology to the public and ASE would help in that goal any way it could.

Chapter 126 – Touchdown

I finally reached the East Coast of the United States. So far it has been smooth sailing, no problems with any of the electronics or propulsion systems. No signs of aircraft, fighter jets, or anything really, except for finally ground after hours of nothing but water.

I would have to pay more attention to the ground, I didn't want to accidentally hit the ground or a tree as I crossed the U.S. on my approach to the Super Bowl stadium.

I continued cranking the tunes on my iPod. As I made my way across the U.S. my excitement, anxiety, and doubt began to grow. Would I really manage to make my dream a reality? It was almost unbelievable to me, my present situation. I was very close to exposing one of the biggest secrets that has ever been kept from humankind.

How did this all end up on my shoulders? How have I managed to become the one who will blow this secret wide open? All I wanted was a flying car, flying cars for everyone. I did not want to go up against the most powerful people in the world. I did not want the deaths of so many people on my conscience, my dad, Emmanuel Goldstein, the 2600 members in the warehouse.

I knew I was doing the right thing but still, all the people who knew about the forbidden technology and yet continued to keep it a secret. Would they all turn on me like a pack of wolves, aim every gun they had against me?

I am a private person, for the most part I prefer to be alone. This thing could make me famous and infamous, a celebrity when all I wanted was my privacy.

Furthermore, to be crass, what was I going to do to make a living? How would I pay the bills? Exposing this technology was not going to provide for me, at least not any way I could figure out. All the forbidden technology would be out in the open. I couldn't get a patent, no one would, which would leave the existing institutional companies, car companies and airplane companies, at a distinct advantage in producing commercial flying cars. I suppose one of those companies could hire me but they wouldn't need to. I could try and start my own company but I had no real money, I would be at a distinct disadvantage compared to the existing players.

I was rapidly approaching the stadium, according to my instruments I was only minutes away. It was go time, let the chips fall where they may.

I just prayed that everything will turn out OK.

I could see the stadium now, I throttled back slowing down as I approached the stadium. I slowly maneuvered over the center of the field, players still running around on the field below. I slowly descended down to the field at the 50 yard line. The action on the field stopped as players and fans looked on in amazement.

I extended the landing gear and landed the craft. I turned on my recorded speech.

"People of Earth..."

Epilogue

Most Effective Electromagnetic Coil Design:

The Boyd Bushman experiment showed that two opposing magnetic fields reduced the effect of gravity on the opposing magnet device: S-N-N-S

I did not have the ability before writing this book to run additional tests. For example would the effect be stronger with a magnet device of: S-N-S-N-N-S-N-S or N-S-S-N-N-S-S-N

Furthermore does the Tesla bifilar pancake coil reduce gravity? I have not tested it so I do not know.

There are several electromagnetic coil designs that need to be tested to see which produce an anti-gravity effect and which design produces the strongest anti-gravity effect.

1. The classic Tesla bifilar pancake coil layered with pancake coil next to pancake coil making a multifilar coil

2. A multifilar coil with Tesla bifilar pancake coils next to mirror versions of the pancake coils.

3. An opposing electromagnetic coil like the Boyd Bushman experiment only using an opposing electromagnet instead of two opposing neodymium magnets. A pattern of:

S-N-S-N-N-S-N-S

4. A layered opposing electromagnetic coil with mirror versions of the electromagnetic coil layers of the pattern: N-S-S-N-N-S-S-N

All these designs need to be tested which could most easily be done in by making the coils for the overunity free energy generator and whichever coil produces the most electricity in the free energy generator would be the best most effective anti-gravity, anti-inertia design.

Most Effective Biefeld-Brown Flat Parallel Plate Capacitor Design:

We know that the higher the voltage the better.

We know from an experiment mentioned in the novel that the higher the pulse rate the better.

Research points to odd nuclear spin materials needing to compose the capacitor plates. It is likely that the higher the odd nuclear spin the better though this has not been studied. Copper has an odd nuclear spin of -3/2, aluminum 5/2, an isotope of titanium 7/2, and bismuth -9/2.

To determine if the capacitor plates degree of odd nuclear spin matters, identical capacitors should be designed using the same thickness and size of the capacitor plates but using different materials for the capacitor plates.

Does a Rotating Mass Effect Gravity:

Mark McCandlish stated that the ARV had a flywheel of some kind. From interviews it is unclear if the flywheel is made of aluminum and rotates underneath the ARV's seats. Aluminum has a very low tensile strength though so if the aluminum disc was a flywheel it could not of rotated at much of a speed. It is also possible that the aluminum disc contained the flywheel or that the flywheel was in the center power amplifier column.

From Bruce DePalma's research, a rotating mass can slow down a clock which indicates increased gravity as the stronger gravity is, the slower the passage of time. But increasing gravity on a craft is probably not desirable unless it can be contained within the crew compartment creating an artificial gravity field letting the crew exist in a gravitational field that keeps their muscles and bones strong.

Furthermore the unreliable testimony of Edgar Fouche stated that there was a rotating mass of mercury in the TR-3B flying triangle and that this reduced gravity on-board the craft substantially. The opposite of what was indicated by Bruce DePalma's research.

Black holes and neutron stars were once just super-massive stars that went supernova expelling lots of matter throughout the cosmos. When this happened the speed at which they rotated increased vastly. Some neutron stars have been clocked with rotation speeds above one rotation per second. To me this suggests that gravity can be increased when rotating matter at very high speeds.

More research needs to be done on rotating masses with and without being composed of odd nuclear spin material and within and without a magnetic field present.

Getroman.com/TV

Made in the USA
Middletown, DE
01 May 2019